Contents

Contents

Anne Brantley
2401 Wentwood Valley Drive # 102
Little Rock, AR 72212-3628

The Long Road Home

The Long Road Home

And Other Short Stories
from Silences in the Gospel of Mark

James S. Lowry

 CASCADE *Books* · Eugene, Oregon

Cascade Books
An Imprint of Wipf and Stock Publishers
199 W. 8th Ave., Suite 3
Eugene, OR 97401

www.wipfandstock.com

ISBN 13: 978-1-62032-400-4

Cataloging-in-Publication data:

Lowry, James S.

The long road home : and other short stories from silences in the Gospel of Mark / James S. Lowry.

xvi + 104 p.; 23 cm—Includes bibliographical references and index.

ISBN 13: 978-1-62032-400-4

1. Short Stories. 2. Bible. N.T. Mark—Homiletical use. 3. Bible. N.T. Mark—Commentaries. I. Title.

BS2585.53 L52 2012

Manufactured in the USA.

For Finn
from his Geppetto

Of such is the Kingdom of Heaven.

And in memory of extraordinary parents,
Rebecca Stallworth Lowry (1912–1996)

What does God require but to do justice,
to love kindness, and
to walk humbly with your God?

and
Bright Anderson Lowry Jr. (1911–1990)

They shall beat their swords into plowshares
and their spears into pruning hooks

Foreword

LIKE PASCAL'S DICTUM THAT love has reasons that reason does not comprehend, Jim Lowry's stories have power that exceed narrative logic. They are thoughtful, thought provoking, not neglecting the mind but challenging it. But it is the heart that counts—or perhaps eyes, eyes that may water enough to make letters of the alphabet look double.

All stories (languages themselves) are filled with gaps. Jim Lowry takes advantage of the gaps in Mark and fills them with inviting language and vivid creativity. Any purist wary that the warning in Revelation 22:18–19 not to add or take away from its words might transfer to Mark need not fret. When Mark says that Jesus reached out and touched a leper, he gives no information about which hand he used. But this does not stop hearers from envisioning Jesus' touch holistically. Filling the gaps happens in two ways. One is to embellish the stories themselves. The other is to tell stories from life in our times that parallel Mark's episodes, parallels that reiterate Mark's plots, characters, and (significantly) settings. One delightful warning: Jim Lowry resorts to common language, very common language, that parallels Mark's to such a degree that it desanctifies and tames the Bible.

Although Jim Lowry's stories from our times are richly autobiographical, both the embellishment of Mark's stories and the modern parallels assuredly have a fictive quality. But this is no obstacle to the truth. Rather, the fictive quality enhances truth. Anyone who hears these stories will recognize what literary critic Erich Auerbach meant when he remarked that all fiction is meant to open up new ways of seeing reality.

Like Jesus' parables, the plots of the stories in this book catch hearers off guard with surprising twists. They first lure hearers into assuming that the events are as ordinarily monotonous as working in a cotton mill. But suddenly the tables are overturned enough to shock even those of us whose hearts are set (hardened) to the point of changing our visions of reality.

Foreword

Like the personages in Mark, the characters in the stories in this book are ordinary, ordinary to the point of being antiheroic. To say this in other terms, like Forrest Gump or Jesus, according to the conventional values of society and culture, they do not excel On the other hand, hearers do not want to miss getting to know these ordinary folk like Skeeter Shiflet or the black man Waterboy, whose real name was Lewis, or Miss Mary Jane Creighton. Unavoidably they clash with problems of evil, people with character flaws, or the demonic in "for God and country," and then do what is right, or either repent or grieve for not doing what is right, and again they shock even those of us whose hearts are set and evoke a new way of living.

Jim Lowry matches Mark's settings in Galilean village life largely with his hometown, Great Falls, South Carolina. But this is Great Falls embedded in a global world, just as Galilee was embedded in systems of the Roman empire. He walks hearers through social crises such as the Civil Rights movement and wars, and once hearers are there, there is no escape from a world tainted with evil. Neither Great Falls or Galilee escapes crashing economies or military disasters. But the tainted world longs to be redeemed. Given the plots and characters, sometimes powers of evil fight back (murderously) against God's grace; at other times there is redemption. God's commonwealth comes to the Old South in Great Falls.

To return to eyes that water enough to make letters of the alphabet look double, I think that Jim Lowry is familiar enough with autobiography to allow me to say that I mean my own.

Robert Brawley

Acknowledgments

My first faltering efforts at writing midrash and naming it as such were for the saints of the Mount Pleasant Presbyterian Church, an old village church near Charleston, South Carolina (1981–1992) and the Idlewild Presbyterian Church in midtown Memphis, Tennessee (1992–1999). For those congregations, on occasion, I experimented with midrash in preaching. Subsequently, those sermons (or versions of those sermons) have been delivered in many other congregations. In all instances, positive responses encouraged me to pursue the art and technique. I am grateful.

I am also grateful to the pastors and congregations of the Riverside Presbyterian Church of Jacksonville, Florida; the First Presbyterian Church of Charleston, West Virginia; the Shandon Presbyterian Church in Columbia, South Carolina; the Covenant Presbyterian Church in Charlotte, North Carolina; and the First Presbyterian Church of Portland, Oregon, who invited me to lead seminars and/or retreats using midrash as a method of Bible study. Many of the stories in this volume have been presented orally at one or more of those events.

From the beginning, when approaching midrash as a method of Bible study, I read a variety of resources, both ancient and modern, from the Jewish tradition. I have been particularly helped and influenced by the work of Rabbi Lawrence Kushner.

I am grateful to friends and colleagues who read early drafts of this book and whose comments have been enormously helpful. They are Erskine Clarke, Wain Wesberry, Douglass Sullivan-Gonzales, Elizabeth Wilson, and Robert Brawley. In addition to making helpful comments on early manuscripts, Robert Brawley has also been kind enough to write the foreword that appears above. In all instances I am grateful. As regards help with this project, in many ways I am powerfully indebted to Sarah Wesberry for contributing her remarkable skills as a copy editor.

Acknowledgments

Above all I am grateful for having been born into a larger family of great storytellers and for having been nurtured in a community of colorful people whose stories have nourished my soul. Without my extended family and without the community of Great Falls, South Carolina, I would have very little about which to spin yarns. The members of my family named in this book are real though the roles they play in the tales may not be. On the other hand, except for my family, characters and stories in this book set in Great Falls, while inspired by real people and real events are, with but a few noted exceptions, entirely fictitious. In the case of the exceptions, the names, save one, have been changed. For all of those who knowingly or unknowingly lent their names and/or personality traits to this volume, I am grateful.

My wife Martha Nichols Lowry has listened patiently to my stories for more than fifty years; our daughters Jayne Stallworth Lowry and Nichols Lowry Malpass have listened to my stories since before they can remember; and our grandson, James Finlay Malpass, will soon, I believe eagerly, take his place in our storytelling tradition. In all instances I am more grateful than I know how to say.

James S. Lowry
Great Falls, SC, 2012

Introduction

THIS BOOK IS NOT a commentary on the Gospel of Mark. To the extent this book is a commentary at all, it is a commentary on what is left unsaid in the Gospel of Mark.

I remember from many years ago an old Garrison Keillor story from National Public Radio's *Prairie Home Companion.* In the yarn, Keillor tells about Midwestern parents who reluctantly and fearfully consent to let their teenage son go to a rock concert. After spending the night camped out in the snow on the steps of the arena so he could be there to get tickets as soon as they went on sale, he came home to find his mother seated at the kitchen table drinking coffee. She and his dad had not slept all night worrying about their son and wondering if they had done the right thing in letting him go to the concert.

His adventure in securing the tickets successfully ended, the son proudly put the tickets on the table in front of his mom and headed off to bed. She then looked at the tickets and looked at the tickets and looked at the tickets. She fingered the tickets. She wondered if she owed it to her son to protect him from the evil concert. She could do just that by seeing that the tickets mysteriously got lost. She trusted her son. Of course she did. He's such a good boy, but what about all those other people who would be at the concert. Could she trust them?

Keillor ended the story without telling us what she did. We are left to wonder, and more importantly, we are left to ponder the implications of the potential alternative ends to the story.

I don't know where Keillor learned that sometimes maddening but often effective literary device. In my view, he easily could have learned it from the person who wrote the Gospel of Mark.

I am not the first, of course, to observe resounding silences scattered throughout Mark. Even though I cannot at all remember now who first introduced them to me, I am certain I did not discover them on my own. Still, I have been reveling in those silences so long I have developed a certain proprietary interest in them. For the last decade or more, I have spent an uncommon (one might say *unholy*) amount of time musing over Mark's gospel, wondering at what I believe are his well-placed silences. My wondering has not been so much in the sense of questioning Mark as the theologian and artist he clearly was. To the contrary, I am held spellbound and struck with awe at what deep truth Mark must have wanted his readers to ferret out on our own in what he left unsaid.

An important word of caution must be offered here. When one becomes intrigued with the silences in Mark, there is a serious temptation to see a lurking void beneath every comma (in the English translations). That seduction must be bravely withstood. The reality is that much (most!) of what is left unsaid in Mark's narrative is likely nothing more than the author's economy of words. As a rule, Mark simply does not give us more detail than necessary or useful for his purpose. In fact, Mark, by far the shortest of the Gospels, is so often scant in detail that on those occasions when the narrative is rich in particulars the reader is put on alert to notice something important in the offing.

Having said that, however, there remains such an impressively large number of places in Mark's account of the gospel where the reader is left to fill in the details that one can only conclude they were put there deliberately.

An early and easily identifiable example of Mark's silences can be found in his account of the temptations of Jesus (1:12–13). Unlike Matthew and Luke, each of whom includes a temptation narrative, Mark does not tell us what the temptations were. Moreover, one must remember Mark predates Matthew and Luke by as much as two decades. That is to say, unlike contemporary readers, Mark's initial audience did not have benefit of Matthew and Luke to fill in the blanks.

To take another and perhaps the most poignant example is to examine Mark's resurrection narrative. Most observers agree Mark ended his gospel at 16:8. That is to say, it is thought vv. 9–19, as they appear in most modern versions, are late additions. That means, in the story as Mark ended it, the women went to the tomb of our Lord, found it empty, and saw a young man dressed in white. The young man tells the women that Jesus, who had been crucified, is risen. The young man then tells the women to go and tell the disciples that Jesus will meet them in Galilee, after which Mark ends his gospel with a strange sentence that says only that the women fled the tomb in amazement and told no one what had happened because they were afraid. The reader is thus left to ponder what the meaning of the resurrection of Jesus might mean.

It is true, of course, in arguing from silence one can never declare with absolute certainty why Mark left so much unsaid. Nevertheless, this book is based on the hypothesis that Mark deliberately left strategically placed silences so his readers would have to wonder what was in them. In the act of wondering, we just might discover ultimate truth, especially if our wondering about what is left unsaid is based on what is said.

For this project, I have identified and chosen six silences in Mark, and I have attempted, with the use of short narratives, to fill those silences. The effort is not to declare with any degree of certainty what Mark left out. Rather, I want to encourage readers to grapple with the implications of a variety of possible ways in which the silences might be filled.

The method I have used in approaching this task is strongly influenced by the ancient rabbinic custom of using midrash wherein, among other things, rabbis spin tales that interpret what for Christians is the Old Testament. The term *midrash* comes from the Hebrew word *d'rash*, which means to examine, to search, or to investigate. It should be pointed out that in common parlance the term is used not only to name a method of interpretation but also to name a product as well as to name a collection. That is, one might say something like *I am going to use midrash to interpret this text*. One might also say something like, *This story is midrash*. By the same token, one might say, *This story is part of the community's midrash* and, in the latter case, have reference to a collection or a library.

Growing out of my initial enthusiasm for the method, the first working title of this book was *Midrash on Mark*. I rejected the title for two reasons. First I quickly learned, from both reading midrash and reading about midrash, that the tradition is so complex, multilayered, and respected in the Jewish community that for me to attempt to replicate it in the Christian tradition could be seen as a kind of presumptuous arrogance I do not wish or intend; second, some of the tales I spin probably exceed the parameters of what is commonly considered midrash. Nevertheless, all of the stories in this book are influenced by that tradition, and all of the stories in this book are slave to the text that inspired them. In it all I have attempted to use two methods often used by Jewish scholars and rabbis in developing midrash. In the first, I will enter the text at the point of its silence and add entirely fictitious details as a method of opening *possible* ways in which the story may have played. Readers are then invited to do the same by developing other possibilities. The point is to encourage readers or groups of readers to grapple with the truth of the text as it is presented.

The second method I use to develop midrash on Mark is to write short stories that are entirely outside the text and separated from it in both time and location. The stories will, nevertheless, and as stated above, be servant of the text and its silence. While many of the characters in these latter tales are based on the lives of real people living in small towns in the southeastern US, except for members of my family, they are either composites of a variety of people or their names, except in a few instances that shall be noted, have been changed to protect their privacy. Some of the stories are autobiographical (or nearly so). In the tradition of midrash, when necessary even those autobiographical stories have been twisted to make them servant of the text. In other words, the effort in the short stories is not to paint an accurate picture of my childhood, my youth, and my family. The effort here is to interpret the texts.

In those instances where colloquial language is used, there is no intent to ridicule. To the contrary, though I deeply value the standard use of language, I have come to recognize that some of our very deepest wisdom and most moving poetry comes from among those whose education has not taken them in the direction of learning the correct use of Standard American English. In these pages there is an attempt to honor that wisdom and poetry.

Such as Psalms —

knowledge is not wisdom

Crossing the Jordan changed people [like death]

one

The Temptations of Jesus
(Mark 1:9–13)

Notes on the Text

MARK'S STORY OF THE temptations of Jesus is part four of a four-part invention that is Mark's rapid-fire introduction to his gospel narrative. Unlike Matthew and Luke, which begin with their respective stories of the birth of Jesus, and unlike John, which begins with setting the story of Jesus in the context of the ordering of the cosmos, Mark begins with a disarmingly simple fragmented sentence. The fragmented sentence (it has no verb) declares that the story about to be told is the good news that Jesus Christ is the Son of God (1:1). Mark then moves, like the others, to an account of the ministry of John the Baptist who came announcing that one greater than he is coming (1:2–8). Then, like Matthew and Luke, Mark gives an account of Jesus' baptism by John in the River Jordan. Mark's account of Jesus' baptism concludes with the voice of God confirming Mark's initial declaration that Jesus is the Son of God (1:9–11). On the heels of that dramatic heavenly announcement comes the present text that is Mark's ever-so-brief account of the forty-day temptations of Jesus. The temptation narrative serves as the last element of the gospel's introduction and opens the way for an account of Jesus' ministry in Galilee before beginning his slow-tread journey to Jerusalem, the city of destiny.

For purposes here, the challenge is that, as noted in the introduction, Mark did not tell us what the temptations of Jesus were. Also as noted in the introduction, it is all but impossible to read Mark's account of the temptations of Jesus without reading into it Matthew's and Luke's accounts.

"midrash — old & new testament"?

The Long Road Home

Readers of Mark must remember it is all but universally agreed that Mark predates Matthew and Luke. In other words, Mark's initial readers did not have access to Matthew and Luke. Mark, it seems, wanted his readers to squirm, wondering what the temptations might have been. Or to state the question more directly, if the Son of God, as the ultimate expression of good news, has been given responsibility for saving the world (i.e., redeeming everything that has ever or shall ever go wrong), how might the Son of God be tempted to pull that off?

Inspired by the ancient use of midrash, in the four tales that follow I have attempted to raise some possible alternative ways to redeem the world. In each instance, the question is this: Might any of these (or other) alternatives have been more alluring to Jesus than dying for the sins of the world? In the first two tales, I playfully enter the text and add entirely fictitious details. In so doing, I take Mark's characters at face value and do not, for example, make any attempt to discuss the nature of Satan or of angels. As a post-Enlightenment person, I am highly suspicious of those who persist in personifying evil. That said, as the well-known preacher Bishop Will Willimon has been heard to say, it is understandable that in our enlightenment we have abandoned talking about devils and demons. The problem, according to Willimon, is that we have not replaced those images with any others that help us talk about the allure of evil in our time. Conversely, the same might be said of shying away from speaking of angels. As for the present exercise, since I shall be entering a first-century document to add fictitious material, I shall when necessary and/or desirable use first-century images to speak of good and evil.

The two remaining stories, while fictitious, are based on experiences taken from my childhood and youth. In one, I serve as the well-intentioned savior figure for my little brother. In the other, an equally well-intended beloved physician serves in that role. It is left to present readers to determine if my suggested acts of redemptions might have tempted Jesus in his quest to redeem the whole creation.

A Tale of Wilderness Wandering

*In those days Jesus came from Nazareth of Galilee and was bap-
tized by John in the Jordan. And just as he was coming up out of
the water, he saw the heavens torn apart and the Spirit descending like a dove on him. And a voice came from heaven, "You are
my Son, the Beloved; with you I am well pleased."*

*And the Spirit immediately drove him out into the wilder-
ness. He was in the wilderness forty days, tempted by Satan; and
he was with wild beasts; and the angels waited on him.*

According to our tradition, on the first night of the thirtieth year of
our Lord, three angels appeared at his chamber door. One angel wore seersucker, the second was in gingham, and the third was dressed in a white
linen suit. When Jesus answered the door, the first angel grabbed Jesus by
the nape of the neck and snarled, "You must come with us. It is time for you
to decide."

"But it's the middle of the night," protested Jesus, "and where are we
going?"

"We have been sent by the Spirit to drive you into the wilderness.
There you must decide by what method and plan you shall save the world."

"Why the wilderness?" asked Jesus.

"Because in the wilderness you will be apart from the empire with all
its principalities and powers. Before you can save the people they must be
delivered from empire. The time has come for you to decide how you will
do that. Our orders are clear. Don't make this any harder than it has to be."

The angels put Jesus on a donkey and drove the donkey to the edge of
the wilderness. "It's time to get off," said the angel in seersucker. He spoke
gently but firmly, as one with authority.

"Alright," said Jesus. "I'll go."

Thus it was Jesus was driven into the wilderness there to decide by
what method and plan the world and all its people would be saved.

On his trek in the wilderness Jesus had to be careful to avoid such
creatures as lions, tigers, and wolves. Not only that, he had to be ever so
careful where he stepped. Once he came within inches of an unfortunate
encounter with a boa constrictor. And yet, all things considered, even the
fiercest of the wild animals were easier to handle than the Roman army of
occupation back in the city; and the monkeys were funny, the robins and
cockatoos were pleasant to watch, the deer and antelope liked to play even
though they were ever so hard to catch, and berries were both plentiful and

delicious. At the end of five weeks, Jesus said to himself, "As long as you stay away from the angry wild beasts, this wilderness experience is not so bad." He had, however, grown quite tired of berries and was getting a little hungry. — *Human*

Then in the early morning of day thirty-six, when Jesus awoke from a restful night's sleep, he saw lurking in the distance a pride of lions who by stealth and raw power were making their way to stalk the oasis where Jesus had stopped to spend the night. If they liked what they saw, which they most certainly would, the lions would surely claim the pool for themselves and keep all others, including Jesus, at bay. Seeing the lions, and afraid of being eaten, Jesus dove into the pool and swam to the middle just out of reach of the fearsome wild beasts. Though safe for the moment, Jesus wondered just how long he would be able to tread water in the face of deadly danger.

Just as Jesus' arms and legs could hold out no longer, from across the wilderness, at breakneck speed, came a handsome rider dressed in black and mounted on a sleek Arabian steed. The powerful animal was as black as the rider's attire. Draped across the horse in front of the rider was the carcass of a freshly killed deer. Horse and rider, with no apparent fear, rode into the middle of the pride where the rider slid the deer to the ground.

Not believing their good fortune, the lions began to devour the deer.

With the lions distracted, the powerful horse was able to wade with his rider to the middle of the pool where the rider held out his hand to Jesus and said, "Satan's the name."

"Jesus of Nazareth," said Jesus as he shook the mysterious rider's hand.

"Let me give you a hand up," said Satan, and with that, he pulled Jesus up behind him, and the powerful horse took Jesus and Satan a safe distance from the lions. Jesus slid off the horse.

"What's a nice boy like you doing out in this godforsaken wilderness?" asked Satan when he had dismounted.

"The wilderness is not godforsaken," said Jesus. "The wilderness is the perfect place for me to figure how best to save the world."

"Save the world?" said Satan. "That's a tall order, but I tell you what. This must be your lucky day. I just happen to be an expert on saving the world."

Satan put his arm around Jesus' shoulder and pulled him close to his side. Jesus could feel the devil's hot breath and smell the devil's musk.

' midRash ' to investigate

"This is what you must do," he said. "Stake out a large territory, one with lots of trees and rivers and lakes, and build a great high wall around it. Be sure the wall has only one gate. In fact, you can call it a gated community if you like. Keep a guard at the gate at all times and don't let human or beast in until they have passed a niceness test."

"Well, what about everybody outside the wall?" asked Jesus. "What will happen to them?"

"Don't worry about them," said Satan. "Just leave them outside, and I'll take care of them."

"I don't think so," said Jesus, "but thank you for rescuing me from the lions."

"Suit yourself," said Satan. He mounted his horse and rode off to the north.

Just then the angel dressed in seersucker came riding up on a donkey. When the angel got to Jesus, he got off the donkey and reached into the saddlebags. From one saddlebag he drew out a loaf of bread. From the other he drew out a jug of wine and a chalice made of earthenware. "Here," said the angel. "Eat this bread and drink this cup."

That's what Jesus did. Refreshed, Jesus went to sleep under a sycamore tree.

On day thirty-seven Jesus was awakened by a wet nose sniffing at his neck just below his ear. When he jumped awake he startled a whole pack of feral dogs who had circled him in the night like so many desperadoes who had been abandoned and left to starve. They began to snarl and growl. The hair stood up on the backs of their necks. In a flash, Jesus climbed the sycamore tree.

Just then, from across the way Satan, dressed in black, came charging up on his big black horse. He cracked a black whip he had taken from his black saddle horn. It sounded like thunder in the dogs' ears and frightened the dogs away. From beneath the tree, Satan held out his hand to Jesus and said, "Here, come take a ride with me."

This time Satan rode Jesus up to a very large building. It was nothing so much as white, except large more even than white. On top of the building there was a sign that said in letters as tall as trees: THE LONG LIFE PRETTY PILL FACTORY.

Again Satan put his arm around Jesus' shoulder and pulled him close. Again Jesus could feel the devil's hot breath and smell the devil's musk.

"I'll tell you what," said Satan. "This really is your lucky day. If you want to save the world, I'll give you the keys to this factory. If you sell a bottle of these pills to everybody, they will live a long, long time. Not only that, for their whole lives they will stay young and pretty, or handsome, as the case may be; and they will follow you anywhere you care to lead them, especially if you make them think the pills are actually working."

"A long time?" asked Jesus. "How long will they live?"

"As long as they keep taking the pills."

"How much do they cost?"

"I don't know," said Satan. "A lot, but you worry too much."

"Then what happens to everybody, and what about those who can't afford the pills?"

"Quit worrying," said Satan. "Just leave them in the wilderness. I'll take care of them."

"I don't think so," said Jesus, "but thanks for rescuing me from the dogs."

"Suit yourself," said Satan, and he mounted his horse and rode off to the south.

Just then the angel dressed in gingham came riding up on a donkey. When the angel got to Jesus, she got off the donkey and reached into her saddlebags. From one saddlebag she drew out a loaf of bread. From the other she drew out a jug of wine and chalice made of earthenware. "Here," said the angel. "Eat this bread and drink this cup." That is what Jesus did.

Refreshed, Jesus went to sleep at the mouth of a cave.

On day thirty-eight Jesus was awakened by two adorable baby bears tugging at his clothes.

"How cute!" said Jesus, and he began to play with the baby bears.

Just then he looked up and coming out of the cave was a very angry mother bear. She was clearly in no mood to compromise. Jesus was about to turn and run for his life when he felt the arm of Satan reach down and swoop him up and put Jesus down behind him on his great black horse.

"My, my, boy," said Satan when they had ridden a safe distance from the mother bear and dismounted, "you do have a way of getting yourself in a mess of trouble with wild beasts.

"I tell you what, boy," said Satan. "This is your last and best chance to get advice from ole Satan on saving the world."

Once again he put his arm around Jesus' shoulder and drew him close; and once again Jesus could feel the devil's hot breath and smell the devil's musk.

"See that machine over there under those oak trees?"

"I sure do," said Jesus.

"Well, I call that ADAM'S ATOM SMASHER. I named it for Adam because he wanted to be like God. ?

"I tell you what I'll do. I'll give you charge of that machine and teach you how to run it. When you know how to smash atoms you can make enough power to make it always daylight for you and everybody who follows you; and you can make it always dark for everybody who doesn't."

"Well, what about the ones for whom it is always dark? What will happen to them?"

"Do you always worry about the losers? Don't worry so much. Just leave the losers in the wilderness, and I'll take care of them."

"I don't think so," said Jesus, "but thank you for rescuing me from the mother bear."

"Suit yourself," said Satan, and he mounted his horse and rode off to the east.

Just then the third angel dressed in a linen suit came riding up on a donkey. When the angel got to Jesus, he got off the donkey and reached into his saddlebags. From one saddlebag he drew out a loaf of bread. From the other he drew out a jug of wine and a chalice made of earthenware. "Here," said the angel. "Eat this bread and drink this cup." That is what Jesus did.

Refreshed, Jesus went to sleep under the stars.

On day thirty-nine, when Jesus woke up there were no wild animals to be seen anywhere. Instead, the three angels came riding up on their donkeys. They were leading behind them a fourth donkey. Saddlebags were draped over the shoulders of the fourth donkey.

"Here," said one of the angels. "Take this donkey and ride her to the west. Ride all day and ride all night. On the fortieth day you will be back in Galilee. In the saddlebags you will find bread and wine. Share it with many people; and, when you have found followers, have them share it with others, and they with still others, and they with others until the whole world will have been invited to eat this bread and drink this cup."

> Now after John was arrested, Jesus came to Galilee, proclaiming the good news of God, and saying, "The time is fulfilled, the kingdom of God has come near, repent and believe the good news."

Another Tale of Wilderness Wandering

In those days Jesus came from Nazareth of Galilee and was bap-
tized by John in the Jordan. And just as he was coming up out of
the water, he saw the heavens torn apart and the Spirit descend-
ing like a dove on him. And a voice came from heaven, "You are
my Son, the Beloved; with you I am well pleased."

And the Spirit immediately drove him out into the wilder-
ness. He was in the wilderness forty days, tempted by Satan; and
he was with wild beasts; and the angels waited on him.

As it happened, Jesus was driven into the wilderness in what looked
like a snow-white chariot, only the chariot had no horses attached. When
Jesus was seated beside the Spirit, she pulled a lid over their heads, locked
it securely, and began to maneuver knobs and levers. Suddenly they were
traveling at breakneck speed to the east. Faster and faster they traveled,
faster than the speed of time.

Finally the Spirit brought the chariot to a stop. When Jesus stepped
out of the time machine, he was seductively greeted by a mysterious woman
seated on the driver's side of a US army jeep. She was dressed in a skin-tight
dress of darkest black. Her long black hair cascaded over her left shoulder.
Her net stockings matched her hair and dress. Her lips were painted crim-
son red. Lips, hair, and dress stood out in stark bold relief to her pale white
skin.

"Welcome to August 1945," she said in a voice that flowed like thick
syrup. "And welcome to Hiroshima. My name is Satan. You must be the one
they call Jesus. I've been expecting you."

"Yes, I'm Jesus," said Jesus, who was all but speechless in the of face
the rubble and twisted metal by which he and Satan were surrounded. "I've
been given responsibility for saving the world. I was driven into this wilderness to consider how best I might do that. Clearly it's not going to be an
easy task."

"Ah," said Satan. "Saving the world is a tall order; but lucky for you,
I have a plan and this particular wilderness is the perfect place to begin."

"How so?" asked Jesus.

"Well sonny boy . . . or should I call you stud man? Well, sonny boy,
this is where the bomb was dropped, and like Adam and Eve eating the for-
bidden fruit, the most powerful empire the world has ever known assumed
the role of God and sealed its pitiful fate.

"Jump in," she said with a smile as she adjusted the black stockings on her shapely legs. "I'll show you around before it's too late."

Jesus got in. Satan drove away. For blocks and blocks they drove. There was nothing but crumbled buildings, one after another. Mingled remains of people and their pets were scattered about the streets like so much roadkill. The people yet standing were the ones unlucky enough to have survive the awful blast. They too were facing near certain death.

Jesus asked Satan to stop. He hung his head from the open jeep and gagged. It was a dry heave. He spewed nothing but yellow bile.

Just then, as if from nowhere, there came a woman carrying a pail of water. She stopped by Jesus, tore a rag from the hem of her kimono, dipped it in the water, and wiped Jesus' face. She again dipped the rag into her pail and then draped it around the nape of Jesus' neck.

"Thank you," said Jesus in voice made raspy by his raw throat.

The woman said nothing as she continued on her way.

From Hiroshima Satan drove Jesus to Nagasaki. In Nagasaki, it was more of the same.

Few words were spoken.

Jesus wept.

At last Satan said to Jesus, "As you can see, it's as you said, saving the world is going to be no small task. See what happens when the empires clash? But cheer up. I too have a time machine. I'll take you for a spin and show you my plan."

Satan took Jesus to the place where her time machine was parked just beside the Spirit's chariot. Unlike the Spirit's snow-white chariot, Satan's time machine was the darkest black. Jesus followed Satan into the cockpit. They took their seats. With her left hand she touched the inside of Jesus' thigh just above the knee. Despite himself, it gave Jesus an all-over feeling, kind of like you have when you first put on silk pajamas. With her right hand she punched in the code for September 10, 1960. At breakneck speed the time machine flew off to the east. Round and round the world they flew, faster than the speed of time. Many thousands of times they sped around the world until the machine came to rest at the top of a great hill.

When Jesus and Satan emerged from the capsule, Satan pointed to the left and said to Jesus, "What do you see?"

"Why I see the two great rivers that surround the garden of Eden; but, unlike in the beginning, there is now in the garden a great city."

? temptation ?

"Yes, that's Bagdad," said Satan, and then she pointed to the right. "And, over there, what do you see?"

"Well, not too much except an endless expanse of desert sand."

"Deceptive, isn't it?" she said. "Beneath that desert sand, just like beneath the garden, is a sea of fossil fuel rather crudely known as crude. It's enough to fuel the world for many generations to come. In fact, at this very moment the leaders of seven nations are meeting in Bagdad. They don't know it yet, but tomorrow they will complete plans for a cartel that will control all of that oil. My plan is give you power over the cartel. With all of that crude under your control, you will have all the power you need to save the world."

"Oh, I don't think so," said Jesus, "but isn't the garden spectacular, even if the city, while beautiful in places, is kind of messy; and the desert, now that I look more carefully, it too is really quite spectacular."

Satan headed toward the time machine. "Come on. We've got lots of time to cover."

"Ok," said Jesus, "but wait just a few minutes. I want to enjoy the view."

"Suit yourself," said Satan with a seductive wink, "but don't make any noises like a female camel."

"Why?"

"Mating season."

"What sounds does a female camel make?"

"If you don't know that you better come with me."

Jesus got back in the time machine. After Satan was settled, she rested her hand slightly higher on the inside of his thigh. Jesus pretended not to notice, but the all-over feeling was getting a little more intense. She crunched in the code for August 1945. Round and round the capsule spun, this time backward around the earth. When they arrived back in Hiroshima, it was 1945 again.

When Jesus emerged from the time machine, there was another jeep parked beside Satan's. A corporal in the United States Army was in the driver's seat. When Jesus got out, the corporal motioned for Jesus to come over. He handed Jesus a small box that was covered in a thin layer of wax.

"What's this?" asked Jesus.

"C rations," said the corporal. "It's about all there is around here to eat that's not contaminated. It's not much but I did manage to find this to go with it."

The corporal reached in the back seat of the jeep and pulled out an ice cold beer.

"Where'd you get that?" said Jesus.

"I'd rather not say," said the corporal. "Eat the C rations and drink this beer."

"Don't you want some?" asked Jesus.

"Just a bite and maybe a sip."

Jesus and the corporal shared the C rations and the beer.

"Rest well," said Satan. "Tomorrow we have more traveling to do."

Jesus didn't rest at all. He spent the night in the makeshift hospital gently rubbing salve on the wounds of the dying.

The next day Jesus and Satan got back in her time machine. This time her hand gradually inched up the inside of Jesus' thigh. Again, Jesus pretended not to notice but had to admit to himself that it felt . . . well, it felt really quite interesting. She set the controls for the spring of 1983. Round and round the earth the capsule spun. When at last they stopped, they were once again on a hill looking over a beautiful valley. Below there was a lake so large you couldn't see the other side. When they got out of the time machine, Jesus' breath was almost taken away with the panorama spread before him.

"Where are we?" asked Jesus.

"This is a land they call Kenya, and that lake is Lake Victoria. It's one of the largest bodies of fresh water in the world. Kenya has just declared this area to be a wildlife preserve. It's called Rama National Park. I brought you here because I propose to give you control of all the fresh water in the world. If you control all the fresh water, you can control all the people. They can't get along without fresh water, you know?"

"Yes, I know," said Jesus. "That's not my style, but can we stay and play with the animals?"

"Whatever," said Satan. She winked at Jesus and adjusted her skirt, which had made its way up her thighs. She went back to the time machine.

As it turned out the laughing hyenas were not as friendly as they sounded and the tigers were not at all as cuddly as they seemed. Jesus soon beat a hasty retreat into the capsule. Satan inched her hand even higher up Jesus' thigh as she set the controls for August 1945.

Back in Hiroshima, when Jesus got out of the machine, there was a general waiting for them. He had four gold stars stamped on his helmet.

"Come with me," said the general. "I've made arrangements for you to sleep in the officers' quarters."

"Thank you," said Jesus. "I am a bit tired. But only for a few hours."

"Rest well," said Satan. "Tomorrow we have more traveling to do."

Grateful for the relative comfort of the officers' quarters, Jesus did sleep a bit. Most of the night, however, he spent at the rim of a mass grave calling the name of each victim as they were being covered with parched earth.

The next day Jesus and Satan returned to the time machine. This time, with her hand fully halfway up the inside of Jesus' thigh, she set the controls for August 2001. Jesus couldn't help but glance down at her hand. Though inexperienced in such matters, he was just beginning to see clearly what she had in mind.

When the machine stopped and they got out, they could barely hear each other talking for all the horns bellowing, brakes screeching, sirens blaring, and people milling about using the F-word over and over in their loudest voices.

"This is New York City," said Satan. "Just look over there." She had to shout in order to be heard above the city's noise.

"I see," said Jesus.

"What do you see?" asked Satan.

"I see two buildings. They're just alike, and they're so tall you have to lean way back to see their tops. They must be almost as tall as the Tower of Babel." *Twin Towers*

"Taller."

"What are they?"

"Together they're called the World Trade Center. Much of the wealth of the world is controlled by people who work in those buildings. I'm thinking of putting you in charge of everything that goes on in there. With you in charge of the world's wealth, saving the world would be a piece of cake."

Satan sidled up to Jesus and slipped her hand in his hip pocket.

Just then a pretty young woman came walking down the street. With two leashes in each hand, she was taking four dogs for a walk all at the same time. No two of the dogs were alike. One was very small with very long hair. Another very tall with very short hair. The third had very curly hair and no tail to speak of. The fourth was tall with a pointy noise and long white hair. When they got near Jesus, he leaned over to pet the one with long hair and a pointy nose.

"Watch it, buddy," said the pretty young woman. "Get your f___in' hands off the dogs. Just who the f___ do you think you are? Do you know whose f___in' dog you just patted on the f___in' head?"

"Bernie Madoff's?"

The dog walker was clearly taken aback. "How'd you know?" she asked.

"It's written right there on his collar."

"Smart ass." And with that, Bernie Madoff's dog raised his leg and peed on Jesus' ankle. Warm dog pee ran into Jesus' shoe. Satan made no effort to hide her sinister smile.

"I don't think this is for me," Jesus said to Satan.

"Suit yourself."

This time, back in the time machine, Satan's hand was almost all the way up Jesus' thigh. Her hand was actually beginning to feel more and more . . . well, more and more . . . pleasant.

With a deep sigh that sounded a little like regret Jesus said to Satan, "Better move your hand."

"What's the matter, big boy? Don't you want to have a little fun."

"Well, yes," said Jesus, "everything you've shown me is quite tempting. In fact, I find you quite tempting, but I'm thinking for the savior of the world to hook up with the powers of darkness doesn't seem . . . well, it doesn't seem quite seemly. No, actually it doesn't seem seemly at all."

"At least I tried," said Satan as she moved her hand and set the controls for the last time for August 1945.

Back in Hiroshima, Satan said, "I give up for now, but I'll be back." She patted Jesus on the butt and gave him a big wink as she strode off to her jeep.

Jesus spent that night playing with the children in a makeshift orphanage. They were not able to sleep because of having bad dreams. Jesus liked the way they snuggled. It made him feel all warm inside and filled him with hope.

Next morning Jesus went back to the Spirit's time machine. When he got in, the Spirit said, "This time you drive."

Jesus set the controls at 0030. Round and round the machine spun to the west until at last it stopped near the Sea of Galilee around about the year 30.

> Now after John was arrested, Jesus came to Galilee, proclaiming the good news of God, and saying, "The time is fulfilled, the kingdom of God has come near, repent and believe the good news."

Hi Ho, Silver! Away!
And May the Good Guys Always Win

Skeeter Shifflet was my younger brother Banks's friend from down the road. Though they were almost exactly the same age, my brother was always about half a head taller than his friend.

Skeeter Shifflet was bad to brag.

"My daddy can whip your daddy with one hand tied behind his back."

Our daddy was not inclined to want to whip anybody, and Banks, more like our father than any of us, knew it. Banks could say nothing.

"My dog can tree a 'coon and mighty near climb up the tree high enough to git him down."

When our neighbor's beagle had puppies, she promised Banks the pick of the litter. Banks chose his puppy for the very reason she was the runt of the litter and would not likely be chosen by anybody else. When she grew up, Brownie delighted in chasing rabbits as was her instinct; but, so far as we ever knew, she never posed a serious threat to a single one of the flop-eared creatures. Banks could say nothing.

"My grandmaw's 'maters are mighty near big as watermelons."

Our Grandmother Lowry grew Better Boys that were unusually large but nowhere near as big as watermelons, and our Grandmother Banks, from whom Banks got his name, delighted in her small cherry tomatoes. Banks could say nothing.

One day when Banks was about four or five years old, which would have put me at about fourteen or fifteen, our father's friend Silas Clarkson showed up in our yard with a horse trailer hitched to his pickup truck. To Banks' great surprise and delight, Silas unloaded a white Shetland pony, which our father had taken in barter from a farmer in the next county.

"Don't know why your daddy wanted this horse," said Silas as he coaxed the animal off the trailer. "He's the stubbornest creature I ever saw." He emphasized the word ever. "Or maybe he's just old and tired."

I took the little horse by the bridle. Silas lifted Banks up on the horse's bare back, and I led him off toward the pasture gate. Silas unloaded the saddle and blanket and walked beside us. Banks could not contain his enthusiasm as he held the mane with both hands.

If the horse had any enthusiasm for what was happening, it was well contained.

"Does the horse have a name?" I asked.

"The man said his name is Silver. I guess his boy thought he was the Lone Ranger or something. I can tell you this much," said Silas Clarkson, "if the real Lone Ranger couldn't have done better than this, he'd have needed a lot more than a faithful Indian companion to save the West. Anyway, the boy who named the horse is off in college now, and I guess his daddy is glad to be rid of one more hay burner."

"This is the stubbornest creature I ever saw," Silas repeated, "and lazy, I reckon."

"I thought Shetland ponies are supposed to be feisty," I said.

"They are," said Silas, "but not this one. He's nothing but stubborn and lazy. Your daddy said just to turn him loose in the pasture for now. He'd see to him when he got home."

That's what we did. When Silver was inside the pasture gate, Silas lifted Banks off his back and I took the bit from the little horse's mouth. Silver eyed the barn and headed straight to it in a lazy trot.

"That's the most energy I've seen come out of Silver," said Silas.

I laughed. Banks was oblivious to our ridicule of his new pet.

"Can I ride him some more?" asked Banks.

"I don't see why not," I said as I took the saddle and blanket from Silas and thanked him. Banks and I made our way to the barn. Silas went back to his truck.

At the barn, I saddled Silver and put the bit back in his mouth. I lifted Banks and put him in the saddle.

"Now all you need is a mask, and you'd be the Lone Ranger," I said to my little brother. "How if I lead him around the pasture for you at first, just until you get used to him?"

That suited Banks fine, and it's just as well. What we learned right off was that, left to his own devices, Silver wouldn't leave the barn at all.

A few days after Silver arrived, Skeeter Shifflet came over to play with Banks. I agreed to saddle Silver so they could take turns riding.

On the way to the barn Skeeter set in with his usual bragging. "My uncle's got a horse twice as big as Silver, and he can run mighty near a hundred miles an hour. The last time I was at my uncle's house I rode that horse until me and the horse both just about fell over from tiredness."

"That so?" I said. "Then you ought not have a bit of trouble with Silver."

Banks couldn't say anything.

I saddled Silver and said, "Ok, company goes first. Skeeter, you get the first turn, but there's just one thing you need to know. Silver has been trained in such a way that it won't do you a bit of good to say any such thing as giddy up. He only goes when you say, 'Hi ho, Silver! Away!' Got that?

"Now, you ride Silver to the end of the lane, wait there for me and Banks, and then Banks can ride him back to the barn."

I lifted Skeeter up on Silver's back, took Silver by the bridle, led him out of the barn and pointed him in the direction of the lane. "Ok, Skeeter, you know what to say."

"Hi ho, Silver," said Skeeter.

Silver just turned his head and looked longingly toward the barn.

"No, it's 'Hi, ho, Silver! Away!'" I said.

"Hi ho, Silver! Away!" said Skeeter in a very mean voice as he dug his heels into Silver's side. Silver did no more than switch his tail and hit Skeeter's leg as though Skeeter were a fly or some other bother.

"You must not be saying it right," I said and took Silver by the bridle and led him across the yard and down the lane with Banks walking beside me. About halfway there, Banks reached up and held my free hand.

At the end of the lane I said, "Ok, Banks, your turn."

I lifted Skeeter down, lifted Banks up, and turned Silver in the direction of the barn.

"Now," I said to Banks, "You know what to say."

"Hi, ho, Silver! Away!" said Banks. Just as Banks said "away," I turned the bridle loose. Silver headed for the barn in a lazy trot.

Twice As Much for a Nickel Too

Pepsi Cola hits the spot.
Twelve full ounces, that's a lot.
Twice as much for a nickel too.
Pepsi Cola is the drink for you.

In our town, for one nickel plus a penny deposit on the bottle, you could get a twelve ounce Pepsi at Hanson's store across from the elementary school playground where the Piggly Wiggly now stands. If you returned the bottle, you got the penny back, or if you preferred you could tell Mr. Hanson you would stand outside, drink the Pepsi before you left, and put the empty bottle in the Pepsi rack and that you would be careful to put it near the other Pepsi bottles so he would not be bothered with having to sort the Pepsi, Royal Crown, Coca Cola, and Nehi bottles. There was no reason for Mr. Hanson to doubt the truth of such a promise.

For two nickels you could get a twelve ounce Pepsi and a Baby Ruth candy bar.

For three nickels you could get into the Saturday matinee at the picture show to see Hopalong Cassidy or Gene Autry or Roy Rogers or my personal favorite, Whip Wilson, plus a cartoon and serial. The serial kept you coming back with three more nickels Saturday after Saturday to see if the hero managed such feats as jumping out of his 1946 Buick convertible before it went over the cliff because the hydraulic brake line had been cut while the hero had been sleeping from the drug that had been slipped into his coffee in a previous episode.

I was lucky. My parents always had three nickels, which they gladly provided to assure that I not miss such excitement.

Some of my friends were not so blessed. If the cotton mills where their fathers and mothers worked were on short time or if one parent or the other had been sick and couldn't work, every nickel counted. More often than not, when times were hard, the Saturday matinee was first to go, no matter that it was unknown whether the hero would find some way to stop his 1946 Buick convertible or jump clear of it before it went over the cliff.

Under such circumstances, nickels thrown from the rolled down window of Dr. Leroy Rataree's maroon 1948 Ford were as welcome as manna from heaven. Dr. Leroy, as he was known, was much admired for his good cheer, his use of big words, and his medical knowledge. He was the only doctor in our town. On many Saturdays, as he drove home for lunch or to make house calls, he made it his practice to throw nickels to the children he saw along the way on the chance it would help them get into the picture show.

For Dr. Leroy to throw nickels out the window of his Ford was, in our town, an unquestioned act of generous and playful kindness that, if nothing else, made children less apprehensive about visits to his office to get stitched up or to have a broken bone set. These many decades later I have not changed my mind on that subject.

And yet, I am haunted by the memory of one Saturday in the fall of 1949 or 1950. I had gotten a ride from my mother as far as the Presbyterian church where she was going to prepare the choir's music for the following day. With the three nickels she had given me in my pocket, I was left with the distance of four or five blocks to walk to the business district where the picture show was located. That far from town, the sidewalks were almost empty, but I did see the black man everybody knew as "Waterboy"[1] walking hand-in-hand toward town with his son Lewis Jr. Since his son is named Lewis Jr., I now take that to mean Waterboy's real name was Lewis Sr. I never knew their last name even though Waterboy worked part-time for my father. When there was a boxcar of supplies for my father's building materials and hardware store to be unloaded, Waterboy would work by the hour after he finished his shift at the mill.

It was well known around town that Waterboy got his name when, as a child, it had been his job to carry buckets of water and a dipper to the cotton fields. When the field hands called out "Waterboy," he would bring them a drink. Without a doubt, he got the job because he was small of stature but strong of limb, characteristics which, like his name, he carried with him to adulthood.

I fell in walking with them.

"Afternoon, Waterboy. Afternoon, Lewis Jr. Mind if I walk with y'all? I'm going to the picture show."

"No, sir, glad to have you. That's where we're goin', too. This here'll be Lewis Jr.'s first time to stay by hisself."

Lewis Jr. must have been five or six. That I called his father, a man the age of my father, "Waterboy" and that Waterboy called me, a child of nine or ten, "sir" says a great deal about the culture in which we lived.

---

1. "Waterboy" is the nickname of a real person in our town. I gave his name to this fictitious person. The episode, while a composite of many real events, is also largely fictitious.

We walked toward town largely in silence. Lewis Jr. and I made a game of not stepping on the cracks in the sidewalk.

Halfway to town, we looked up from our game in time to see Dr. Leroy's maroon Ford coming toward us with the window rolled down. Sure enough, just as he got beside us, he blew the horn and tossed two shiny nickels out the window. They landed on the sidewalk just in front of us. I ran to pick up mine. As I stood up I could see Lewis Jr. was looking up at his father. Waterboy shook is head so slowly and so slightly that the movement could hardly be seen. I picked up the other nickel and held it out to Lewis Jr. He looked up at his father again. Again his father moved his head so slightly and so slowly the movement was barely perceptible.

I said nothing and put both nickels in my pocket. We walked on to town in silence.

At the picture show I paid my fifteen cents to Miss Martha Ann in the ticket booth and waited for Lewis Jr. to pay his fifteen cents. Before he stepped up to the window, Waterboy leaned over, held out his hand, and said to his son, "Here's another nickel for you to buy some popcorn."

I went inside glad for the extra two nickels to buy popcorn and a Pepsi. I sat downstairs as was the custom for white people in those days. Lewis Jr. bought his ticket, went inside, bought his popcorn, and went upstairs to sit in the balcony.

two

Demons Know Best (Mark 4:35—5:13)

(See also Mark 1:21–28)

Notes on the Text

FOR UNDERSTANDABLE REASONS, MARK'S account of Jesus calming of the storm (4:35–41) and Mark's account of Jesus casting the legion of demons out of the demented man (5:1–13) are almost always treated separately. Indeed, on some levels, it is perfectly reasonable that those who organized the Christian cannon of Scripture into chapters and verses made a chapter break between the two stories. That is, in current versions, the calming of the sea is in one chapter and the casting of demons into the sea is in another. Contemporary readers, however, should remind themselves from time to time that Mark and the others who wrote or compiled the original texts that are the Bible made no such numerical divisions. While obviously helpful as navigational tools, the divisions can be a distraction.

For example, taken together, the present stories provide both an important comparison and an important contrast to each other that we can be sure Mark did not want us to miss. In the one instance, Jesus calmed the angry storm that was raging around the disciples; and in the other instance, Jesus calmed the angry storm that was raging inside the demented man. Similarly, in the first instance, the disciples wondered, "Who . . . is this?" (4:41); and by stark contrast, in the other instance, the man possessed by a legion of demons said, "What have you to do with me, Jesus, Son of the most high God?" (5:7). In other words, those closest to Jesus didn't really know him but the powers of darkness did. By Mark's observation, the disciples didn't get it, but the demons did. The contrast becomes all the more compelling when one remembers that it is widely agreed among scholars that anytime in the Gospel of Mark you read the word *disciples* you can substitute the word *church* and not be far off the mark. In other words, in Mark's view the church doesn't really know who this man Jesus is but the powers of darkness do.

As to the former, the question of why disciples (church!) don't recognize Jesus will not be dealt with specifically in this context. Without a doubt that issue is a (some would say *the*) recurring theme throughout Mark's gospel and is clearly the big issue over which Mark wants the church to squirm. In some ways it is the question that underlies all of the tales in this book. Nevertheless, for purposes of this chapter, it is the more narrowly focused question of how the powers of darkness recognize Jesus that interests us. It does so for the very reason that on that subject, like on so many others, Mark is tantalizingly silent. He simply doesn't tell us how the demons knew the identity of Jesus. We're left to speculate. My strong hunch is that Mark's intent is that in speculating, even if we don't discover *how* the demons know who Jesus is, we'll discover that they always do. In other words, in our wondering *how* they know we'll discover that the powers of evil not only recognize Jesus, but they are always mortally threatened by the ultimate powers of good embodied in him and in his faithful followers.

As in the last chapter, the observation of Bishop Willimon will be followed. That is to say, the issue of "enlightened" people personifying the powers of evil will not be parsed. The assumption here is that the power of evil exists in the world and some language is needed to discuss that power. If we spend all our time and energy arguing over whether or not demons actually exist, we'll surely miss the powerful punch of texts like the present one.

In the tales that follow, the effort is not so much to explain *how* the powers of darkness recognize the power of God but to point out that the powers of darkness always will recognize God's power, will always be threatened by God's power, and will always fight against but ultimately be defeated by God's power. As before, in the first two I playfully enter Mark's narrative and provide additional entirely fictitious material. The two other short stories are based on experiences in my youth growing up in a small Southern town. The hope is that readers will be encouraged to see many instances from their own experience where the powers of evil have been threatened and overcome by the power of this man Jesus and his followers.

The Powers of Darkness Grim

On that day, when evening had come, [Jesus said] to [the disciples], "Let us go across to the other side." And, leaving the crowd behind, they took him with them in the boat, just as he was. Other boats were with them. A great windstorm arose, and the waves beat into the boat, so that the boat was already being swamped. But he was in the stern, asleep on the cushion, and they woke him and said to him, "Teacher, do you not care that we are perishing?" He woke up and rebuked the wind, and said to the sea, "Peace! Be still!" Then the wind ceased, and there was a dead calm. He said to them, "Why are you afraid? Have you still no faith?" And they were filled with great awe and said to one another, "Who is this that even the wind, and sea obey him?"

When he stepped out of the boat, immediately a man out of the tombs with an unclean spirit met him. He lived among the tombs; and no one could restrain him any more even with chains; for he had often been restrained with shackles and chains, but the chains he wrenched apart, and the shackles he broke in pieces, and no one had the strength to subdue him. Night and day among the tombs and on the mountain he was always howling and bruising himself with stones. When he saw Jesus from a distance, he ran and bowed down before him and shouted at the top of his voice, "What have you to do with me, Jesus, Son of the Most High God? I adjure you by God, do not torment me." For he had said to him, "Come out of the man, you unclean spirits!" Then Jesus asked him, "What is your name?" He replied, "My name is Legion, for we are many." He begged him earnestly not to send them out of the country. Now there on the hillside a great herd of swine was feeding, and the unclean spirits begged him, "Send us into the swine; and let us enter them." So he gave them permission. And the unclean spirits came out and entered the swine and the herd, numbering about two thousand, rushed down the steep bank and into the sea, and were drowned in the sea.

With such heavy loses from what came to be known as the Slaughter of the Guilty, an emergency meeting of the Council of Demons was called for the very night in which 2000 true and patriotic spirits of darkness eagerly jumped to their deaths in the face of relentless good. The meeting was held in the outer chamber of hell just east of the western gate. A delegate from each of seven tribes was present. Both the delegates and the tribes they represented were named for what were commonly known as The Seven Deadly Sins, though every indecent demon well knows there are sins more deadly by far than, for example, sloth or lust. Still the tribes had to be named something and names like Genocide and Exploitation don't have much of a ring to them. In truth, however, each of the seven tribes was well armed with demons of the most deadly sort. Moreover, in each of the more deadly sins, there was an element of one or more of the more famous seven.

When Anger, who was high priest that year, had called the meeting to order, he said, "Alright, ladies and gentlemen . . ." But before he could continue, Envy was on her feet.

"I object. There are neither 'ladies' nor 'gentlemen' present. We are all either male demons or female demons."

"I stand corrected," said Anger with fire in his eyes, "but this is an emergency. We don't have time for internal bickering. The very existence of evil as we know it is at stake."

"Here, here," shouted the others in near unison. Envy took her seat but she was clearly not happy. Wrath put an understanding arm around Envy's shoulder.

"It's time for decisive action," said Greed. "If we don't act quickly, the forces of good will get out of hand and soon be out of control. Who knows? We could be faced with a serious outbreak of peace, harmony, and good will."

"Here, here," shouted the assembly.

"Let's storm the barricade and carry off their women, dress them like rabbits and send them back to ply their trade," said Lust, who had come to the meeting, as was his custom, breathing heavily.

Envy was on her feet in a flash, but before she could speak Anger said, "Sit down, Envy. This is more serious than a bunny hop . . . no pun intended."

Still on her feet, Envy shouted, "You're all sexist pigs"

"Of course we are," said Gluttony under his breath. "It's our nature to be pigs. Our comrades lost their lives as pigs." As he spoke his heavy jowls shook like a bowl full of jelly.

"Let's all calm down," said Sloth who, in all matters great and small, preferred to take the line of least resistance. "Since, as you may have observed, I am much less hyper than the rest of you, while you were emoting I was able to reflect on the problem. I believe I have thus come up with a solution.

"Male and female demons," he said glancing with raised eyebrow in the direction of Envy, "we have one great advantage over the followers of this man Jesus."

"Oh?" said Anger. "And what might that be?"

"It's simple," said Sloth. "We know who he is. We may not know exactly what good is, but we know it when we see it. Good is the enemy, and this Jesus is good . . . pure, raw good, I tell you. 'Rise, take up your bed and walk . . . your faith has made you whole,' 'Do it unto the least of these,' 'turn the other cheek,' and all the rest. This man Jesus is good, I tell you, but we have the advantage. We know it but the others, even his followers, don't have a clue."

Suddenly, the members of council were all ears. "Go on," said Pride, who would have much preferred to have had the idea himself.

"Well, first of all," said Sloth, "no more grandstand plays . . . no more invading some poor sucker and making a wild person out of him. You see what that got us. We have to be more subtle than that. Since we know who Jesus is and they don't, it'll be easy and won't take much energy at all."

Sloth was well known for not wanting to expend much energy.

He went on. "All we have to do is quietly plant our seeds first among the leaders of the synagogue, then among the leaders of the palace, and at last among the disciples of this man Jesus, known to himself and to us as the son of God. After that, all we have to do is sit back and watch them do our dirty work for us."

The assembly fell silent.

"Go on," said Gluttony as he wiped the gravy from his chin. "You may be onto something."

"It's simple," said Sloth, who was being uncharacteristically animated. "Pride and Envy, you and your hordes will be key players in the operation . . . on the frontline, as it were. First, Pride, you must send a few of your most devious operatives to the synagogue. Dress the priests like peacocks. Then move on to the palace, and do the same there among the politicos. At last, move among the disciples and make them wonder who is greatest among them.

"Then, Envy, it'll be your turn to have your forces filter in . . . not too many . . . just a few of your best and brightest. Keep it a covert operation. All you have to do is make priests and Levites jealous of each other. Do the same for the officers of the court from the emperor and governor on down. Saturated with pride and envy, they'll not recognize good when they see it.

They'll only see the one completely good person as a threat to the way they do business. Then all you have to do is move on and do the same among his followers."

"Ah," said Envy, "I see where you're going. We get the holy people to join hands with the empire to destroy good."

"Exactly," said Sloth. "Meanwhile, Lust, it'll be your job to keep the disciples of Jesus distracted first with doubts about their own raw feelings and then with suspicion and curiosity about each other's practice in the bed. First thing you know, all they'll focus on or talk about is sex. That way, good both in and around them will go wanting, but more than all of that, Lust, you'll breach their defenses so Anger, Greed, and Gluttony can move in to seal their fate and assure they do our dirty work for us. Why, who knows? If we play our cards right, we might even get one of them to play footsy with the governor to betray Jesus. Since they don't really know who he is, when the jig is up, they'll run and hide. Mark my word."

There was a moment of reflective silence. Then gradually the room began to buzz. Finally Anger spoke. "Denizens of the underworld, brave and true, I do believe we have a plan. Do I have a motion?"

The vote was unanimous. As the powers of darkness grim filed out of the meeting room and made their way through the streets of hell they could be heard to sing:

Ho hi, ho hi,
We're off to watch him die.
If we dig, dig, dig
at the rich, rich, rich
They'll do our dirty
tricks, tricks, tricks.
Ho hi, ho hi,
We're off to watch him die
With an end to good
As we understood,
Hope will soon
be nix, nix, nix.
Ho-hi, ho-hi, ho-hi-ho-hi-ho-hi.

The Powers of Darkness Grimmer than Grim

On that day, when evening had come, (Jesus said) to (the disciples), "Let us go across to the other side." And, leaving the crowd behind, they took him with them in the boat, just as he was. Other boats were with them. A great windstorm arose, and the waves beat into the boat, so that the boat was already being swamped. But he was in the stern, asleep on the cushion, and they woke him and said to him, "Teacher, do you not care that we are perishing?" He woke up and rebuked the wind, and said to the sea, "Peace! Be still!" Then the wind ceased, and there was a dead calm. He said to them, "Why are you afraid? Have you still no faith?" And they were filled with great awe and said to one another, "Who is this that even the wind, and sea obey him?"

When he stepped out of the boat, immediately a man out of the tombs with an unclean spirit met him. He lived among the tombs; and no one could restrain him any more even with chains; for he had often been restrained with shackles and chains, but the chains he wrenched apart, and the shackles he broke in pieces, and no one had the strength to subdue him. Night and day among the tombs and on the mountain he was always howling and bruising himself with stones. When he saw Jesus from a distance, he ran and bowed down before him and shouted at the top of his voice, "What have you to do with me, Jesus, Son of the Most High God? I adjure you by God, do not torment me." For he had said to him, "Come out of the man, you unclean spirits!" Then Jesus asked him, "What is your name?" He replied, "My name is Legion, for we are many." He begged him earnestly not to send them out of the country. Now there on the hillside a great herd of swine was feeding, and the unclean spirits begged him, "Send us into the swine; and let us enter them." So he gave them permission. And the unclean spirits came out and entered the swine and the herd, numbering about two thousand, rushed down the steep bank and into the sea, and were drowned in the sea.

At the news of the tragic deaths of 2000 of their number, even as the elfin demons were dancing through the streets of Hell singing their Ho-Hi, Ho-Hi song, old Satan him-and-herself began descending the brimstone steps of Hell. One story down, two stories, three stories down, down, down, down, went Satan until she-and-he, at seven stories down, had reached the hallway of Hell's deepest chamber. It was there, in the darkest of darkness, that the most vile, sinister, and grim demonic forces of evil were kept. Even by the standards of Hell, such powers were so sinister their personas had to be kept in cages. As he-and-she expected, Satan found the darkest powers of darkness picking their noses and scratching their arses.

Unlocking their cages, she-and-he summoned the grimmest of the grim to a meeting room lit with torches. It was at the end of the corridor in Hell's deepest chamber. There was much growling and snarling, poking and jabbing, which is the way of the grimmest of the grim and is exactly why Satan kept them in cages until he-and-she had an assignment for them.

"Alright, alright, settle down," said Satan in her-and-his most sinister and commanding voice. "I have an assignment for you."

"Well, it's about time," said DeForested Morass.

"I should say," said Fore Closure.

"Well," said Satan, "I think you'll like what I'm about to say and you'll agree the caper will prove to be well worth the wait."

"We're listening," said Hopeless Addiction as he dug a ball of wax from his ear and flicked it across the room. Splat, it hit the wall. "I suppose this has something to do with 2000 demons joyfully jumping to their deaths in the face of the unabashed good in the person of one Jesus of Nazareth?"

"Yes," said Satan, "I see you've heard our tragic news."

"Heard? Of course, we've heard," said Economic Collapse.

"Such news travels fast along the corridors of Hell," added Fanatical Religion in a voice that was like syrup being poured over burning coals. Fanatical Religion was so blind he had to be led around by the hair of his head. No Doubt was usually assigned the task.

"Enough," said Satan. "Here's the plan."

"We're listening," repeated Hopeless Addiction sarcastically as he dug a ball of wax from his other ear and flung it across the room. It landed in Corporate Greed's perfectly coiffed hair causing her to curse loudly. All others burst out in peals of sinister laughter at the sight of Corporate Greed picking earwax out of her bouffant.

As their laughter faded, Satan began to lay out his-and-her plan.

"As it happens," said Satan, "your lesser colleagues from the Council of the Tribes of the Seven Deadly Sins have devised a plan . . . a penny-ante plan it may be, but a plan nonetheless."

"Yes, we expected as much," said Power Lust. "Their silly singing echoed all the way down here."

"Trivial their plan may be," said Satan, "but it will keep mortals stirred up, by my estimate, for about two millenia especially since, at best, only the best of his followers have as much as a half-baked notion of who this Jesus is.

"And that's when you come in."

"Oh, yeah? How so?" asked Military Complex coming up for air. She was in the back of the room making out with Industrial Giant.

"Two thousand years is about how much time it will take mortals to amass enough power and know-how to destroy their world and themselves with it. Soooo, two thousand years after Jesus the Good has gone back to be with his Da-da, I will turn you loose to invade the earth. All you have to do is to keep the mortals who think they know Jesus so preoccupied with their internal bickering that they will be unwilling and unable to call the hand of evil. That way, nothing that has ever gone wrong in the empire, in the market, or for that matter in any of their silly religions, will ever be redeemed. Soon after, very soon, when the empires, markets, and religions are powerless, the whole human experiment will implode."

"That's it?" asked Global Warming.

"That's all we have to do?" asked Power Lust.

"You sure there's nothing else?" someone else chimed in.

"Piece of cake!"

"A walk in the park!"

The Powers of Darkest Darkness Grimmer than Grim were beside themselves with excitement. Military Complex and Industrial Giant were breathing heavily and tugging at each other's clothes.

"But two thousand years? That's a long time," said Power Lust. "I'm not sure I can wait two thousand years."

"Don't worry," said Satan. "To paraphrase one of their poets, 'Two thousand years in the sight of evil is as but day before yesterday when it is passed.' Now, return to your cages. I'll be back to get you in exactly two millennia. At that time it will be your job to assure that by reason of inaction among the faithful in matters that matter, all mortal hope for a new earth will be destroyed and any dreams they may foster for a new heaven shall be, shall we say, tarnished. Then we'll see what comes of this Jesus they think they know: riding his flop-eared donkey / clippity-clop, clippity-clop, / through this village, past that shop / saying eat this bread, drink this cup."

The swineherds ran off and told it in the city and in the country.
Then people came to see what it was that had happened.

The Methobapterian[1]

Preacher Edwards was, by birth, training, and profession a Methodist. His thick shock of snow-white hair, perpetually ruffled trousers, slightly soiled white shirt, and well-worn but highly polished black shoes made him look the part.

Preacher Edwards served the Methodist church in our town for many more years than was usual for Methodist pastors, especially among those serving small congregations in small towns. Every three or four years, and more often if necessary, at the will of the bishop and district superintendent, on a rotating basis, there would be a fruit-basket turnover resulting, on a specified day in June, in great movement among Methodist preachers. Not so for Preacher Edwards. Every year, just before time for moves to be announced, the good Methodists in our town would raise such a ruckus wanting Preacher Edwards to stay, the bishop would finally say, "Well, alright. One more year but next year . . ." Then the next year it would be the same until finally Preacher Edwards was able to stay in our town until he retired. In fact, he stayed in our town for many years after he retired, though it was well known he was careful to stay out of the way of the string of young preachers who followed him. After he retired, anytime a Methodist asked him to conduct a wedding or baptism or funeral, he always said something like, "Nope. Have to give these young preachers a chance to find their way."

Since after retirement he was largely inactive in the Methodist Church, that's when he earned the title Methobapterian. He got that title because he soon became the substitute preacher of choice for every church in town when one of the preachers turned up sick on Sunday morning or wanted to take a few days of what they thought of as well-earned vacation. Thus it was that everyone in town, at least all the churchgoing people in town, and that was almost everybody, got to know Preacher Edwards' much beloved

1. This tale is entirely fictitious. The Methobapterian (including his title, his physical appearance, and his idiosyncratic gestures) is, however, based on Rev. J. Y. Cooley, who for many years served the Mount Dearborn (United) Methodist Church in Great Falls, South Carolina. In the tale, the actions of the Methobapterian at the school board meetings and at the Great Falls schools were inspired by similar actions taken by Rev. J. Philips Noble, who was pastor of the First Presbyterian Church of Anniston, Alabama at the time the Greyhound bus carrying freedom riders was burned just outside that city, and by Rev. Paul Tudor Jones who was pastor of the Idlewild Presbyterian Church in Memphis, Tennessee, at the time of the sanitation workers' strike and the assassination of Dr. Martin Luther King Jr. The influence and impact of these three giants of the faith on their communities and on me are beyond measure.

idiosyncracies. For example, when he was about to make a really strong point in a sermon about some sin or other, he would pop his lips together four or five times in rapid succession, or he would put his right hand in his pocket and rattle his change, or sometimes he would do both at the same time. By contrast, when something made him especially happy or he was about to say something that was full of grace, his eyes danced and his feet did a little shuffle. It was almost like a soft-shoe, but neither foot actually left the floor.

In the years immediately after the Supreme Court's decision in *Brown v. Board of Education*, Preacher Edwards and his role as a Methobapterian served our town well. It was during those years that every school board in the South had to come to terms with the law of the land. School board meetings in our town, like everywhere else in the region, were tense. During that time, Preacher Edwards made it his business to attend every meeting of the board. He never spoke. He just sat there with his thick shock of snow-white hair, in his ruffled trousers, his slightly soiled white shirt, and his well-worn but highly polished black shoes. That is to say, he never spoke any words; but when it came time for public comment and someone would stand up and say something stupid or mean like, "I don't care what they say, my boy ain't going to school with no n___s," Preacher Edwards would slide his steel folding chair across the floor just enough to make a terrible racket. Or when someone would say something like, "What's going to happen when it's time for the Junior-Senior Prom . . . it ain't right for n____s and whites to dance together," Preacher Edwards would pop his lips and rattle his change.

Months went by with no decision being made about how the schools would integrate. Finally J. R. Melvin came to the board with a proposal. He copied it after what he had heard other school boards had done. When he proposed that in the first year twelve volunteers from the black school be allowed to go to the white school and the next year twenty-four and the year after that thirty-six, Preacher Edwards slid his chair across the floor, popped his lips and rattled the change in his pocket. By that time, Clarence Powers, chair of the board, had had enough and said, "Preacher Edwards, if you don't sit still, I'm going to have to ask you to leave."

The Methobapterian said, "Sorry, Clarence, I have a few nervous habits. Mrs. Edwards says they're about to drive her crazy."

"I bet they are," said Clarence. Still J. R.'s proposal got voted down by a vote of five to one.

At the next meeting of the school board, Peggy Prescott, who had been chair of the Pastor Relations Committee of the Methodist Church for most of the time Preacher Edwards had preached there, stood before the board to make a proposal. Peggy proposed that they take one school and make it grades one through six and the other school and make it grades seven through twelve and that teachers and students be assigned to classes without regard to race. Whether Preacher Edwards had discussed that idea with Peggy beforehand no one ever knew for sure, but after she sat down, those sitting close to Preacher Edwards could see his eyes dance, and many more in the room heard as his feet made a little shuffle. It was almost like a soft-shoe only he never left his chair and his feet never left the floor.

There were many details that had to be worked out, but that's basically what the board decided.

The year the plan was implemented, on the first day of school, our town's Methobapterian was seen sitting on the steps of the high school when the students arrived. There he was, just sitting with his shock of thick snow-white hair and ruffled trousers, reading the morning paper like it was the most natural thing in the world for a white-haired old preacher to be sitting on the steps of the school house reading the paper. As unusual as it was for him to be there, no one questioned it. Of course, everybody with a brain in their head knew why he was there. If one of the students or teachers spoke to him, he spoke back, but he didn't look up from his paper. Other than rattling his paper, the only sound he made was when his feet did a little shuffle that was almost like a soft-shoe, only his feet never left the steps. Because of the bus schedules, the elementary school day didn't begin until forty-five minutes after the high school day began. That gave Preacher Edwards just enough time to drive his white 1949 Ford sedan across town so he could be on the steps of that school reading the funny paper when the younger students arrived.

Preacher Edwards kept at that morning routine for the first week or two of the school year. He didn't miss a day, not even the day it rained cats and dogs just as school was taking in. He sat there with the paper in one hand and the big black umbrella he used for rainy day funerals in the other.

And, of course, as had always been his custom, on Friday nights he was at the home football games; but for the first few years after the schools were integrated, he also traveled with the team and, in all instances, he sat just behind the cheerleaders. His thick shock of snow-white hair, ruffled trousers, and well-worn but highly polished black shoes made quite a contrast to the perky young cheerleaders who, for the first time ever, came in a variety of skin tones.

It would, of course, be singularly untrue to claim that the first years of integration in our schools were all sweetness and light. There were tense moments as students who had lived their whole lives within a few miles of each other came together from two very different cultures. Still, the demons of racism were largely kept at bay, and the school years passed without serious incident.

The Cake Lady and Beaufort Junior Johnson[2]

There were exactly fifty-two members of the Great Falls High School Class of 1952. Charlene Monroe, who had been to Ridgecrest Baptist Assembly Grounds three summers in a row, was president of the class. From something she had learned at Ridgecrest, Charlene saw it as a sign that the number in the class matched exactly the number of the year. She was certain an omen requiring faithfulness could be worked out by using numbers found in the book of Revelation if somebody just knew how to do the math. At the first class meeting of their senior year when it was learned that Mary Jane Floyd had turned up in a family way and dropped out of school leaving exactly fifty-two members of the class of '52, Charlene suggested that God was using Mary Jane's misfortune to caution the class. She suggested they call themselves "The Faithful Fifty-Two" and vow to be faithful to each other and to Great Falls High as long as they lived. There was a brief argument put forth by some that it was not God who got Mary Jane in a family way and "Fighting Fifty-Two" might have a better ring to it than "Faithful Fifty-Two." But, because of its religious overtones, in the end Charlene's suggestion seemed pleasing to the class. In testimony of their vow of faithfulness, for that whole year every time the Great Falls High School alma mater was sung, no matter whether it was at a ball game or in an assembly, when the last line of the anthem, ". . . the greatest, grandest, best of all, our alma mater!" had been sung to the tune of "Stars and Stripes Forever," the senior class shouted, *Yea, Faithful Fifty-Two! We'll Forever Be True to You!*

On graduation night, only fifty-one of the Faithful Fifty-Two marched down the aisle of the Great Falls High School auditorium. I counted them. I was sitting in the front row of the auditorium just behind my mother who was playing the piano for the occasion. While she played "Pomp and Circumstance" with as much pomp and circumstance as she could pound out of the old Thompson upright, adding variety now and then to the old Edward Elgar tune by playing the treble clef an octave higher than it is written and bass clef an octave lower, I counted: Forty-nine, fifty, and Ernie Yerkes made fifty-one.

2. While this story is based on real events, the character of the Cake Lady is a melding of two strong women in my hometown. One did in fact bake and sell cakes. She would never, however, have slain the king's English. The other, when she was widowed, ran a small neighborhood store from the front room of her house in one of the mill villages of our town. Childless herself, she became mother figure for many of the children who lived in that village.

I knew exactly which member of the class was missing.

Buford Junior Johnson, though he was an honor student, wasn't there. He didn't march down the aisle; he didn't sit with the others; his name was not called by Mr. Tom Purser, principal of Great Falls High School; he did not walk across the stage to get his diploma in a plastic protective folder with a seal of Great Falls High School on it from Mr. Lewis Merewether Clark, county superintendent of schools, and at the end of the ceremony, he didn't move the tassel on his cap from one side to the other when Charlene Monroe gave the cue so they would all do it at the same time. Not only that, after all the speeches had been made and everyone stood while my mother played a stirring rendition of "Stars and Stripes Forever" for the class to sing the alma mater, after they had sung, ". . . the greatest, grandest, best of all, our alma mater," no one shouted a pledge of faithfulness forever. Whether that was because of the solemnity of the occasion or the absence of Beaufort Junior Johnson is not known.

Junior is Beaufort Junior Johnson's real middle name. It's the middle name his daddy, Big Beaufort Johnson, gave him, so that's what Dr. Leroy Rataree wrote on the birth certificate on the night Beaufort Junior was born. Big Beaufort was just that proud to have a son. The new daddy named his son like he did with no thought of naming him Beaufort Earl Johnson Jr. I guess Big Beaufort figured if he named the boy Beaufort Junior and called him by both names as is often done, especially in the South, everybody would always know who's son he was.

When Beaufort Junior got to be a famous pastry chef in New York City, he had come to be known as B. J. Johnson. By that time Big Beaufort was again proud of Beaufort Junior. Like when he was born, Big Beaufort bragged about Beaufort Junior all over Great Falls to anybody who would listen.

"Of course you know Beaufort Junior's baking bread for the Waldorf-Astoria now."

"Got a letter from Beaufort Junior the other day. He baked the cake for a big reception they had at Rockefeller Center. Ike and Mamie Eisenhower was there."

He said Ike and Mamie like they were Beaufort Junior's closest and dearest friends.

As proud as Big Beaufort was of Beaufort Junior when he was born and as proud as he finally became of Beaufort Junior again, there was one long, dark night when Big Beaufort Johnson was crazy with grief and shame over Beaufort Junior Johnson. That long night was followed by two more long weeks of fear for Beaufort Junior's safety.

The night of Big Beaufort's grief and shame was in the late spring of 1952, just two days before high school graduation. Late that afternoon, right before dark, Beaufort Junior Johnson left the cake lady's house, delivered a pineapple upside-down cake to Miss Alberta Jones at Alberta's Ready to Wear, went home, hit his daddy up beside the head with a flower pot, left him out cold on the floor, went back to the cake lady's house, and told her what he had done. My mother and I happened to be at the cake lady's house when he arrived. We were there to pick up two lemon meringue pies that my mother planned to serve at her bridge club the next afternoon. I had jumped out and run to the door with my mother close behind. I was in hopes of a treat that almost always came as part of each delivery from the cake lady's kitchen.

"Lena Pearl," my mother said to the cake lady when she saw the pies with their meringue light brown and piled high, "you've outdone yourself again. I don't know how you do it."

Just then is when Beaufort Junior Johnson burst into the kitchen all red in the face and out of breath. "I hit Daddy up beside the head with a flower pot, and he's out cold on the floor," he said with no thought what so ever given to my mother and me being present.

"You did what!" exclaimed Ms. Lena Pearl Montrose.

Everybody in Great Falls knew Ms. Lena Pearl Montrose as the cake lady. She was famous all over the county for her pineapple upside-down cakes, her lemon meringue pies, and her yeast rolls. She sold her cakes and pies for $2.00 each and her yeast rolls for $2.00 a dozen or $3.00 for two dozen. She made a pretty good living at it ever since her husband, Leonard Montrose, had died of a heart attack ten years earlier while hunting rabbits and squirrels down by Debutary Creek. It was said in Great Falls that a church supper wasn't worth going to if nobody had thought to bring one of Ms. Lena Pearl Montrose's pineapple upside-down cakes. It didn't matter whether it was Methodist, Baptist, Presbyterian, Holiness, or Episcopalian. The cake lady was a Baptist. We were Presbyterians.

Beaufort Junior Johnson knew the cake lady well. In the afternoons after school and on Saturday mornings it was his job to help the cake lady with her baking. One thing he did was to go by Jack Thompson's liquor store to get cardboard boxes to cut up and cover with waxed paper so Miss Lena Pearl could turn her upside-down cakes upside-down on something that would not have to be returned. She had lost some of her best china plates which she had gotten as bonuses from Joe Prichard's pure oil station. Sometimes her customers would forget to return her dishes, and they got mixed in with the ones they had gotten as bonuses from Joe Prichard.

It was also Beaufort Junior's job to wash the cast iron skillets in which the cake lady baked the pineapple upside-down cakes. He had to be careful never to wash them in hot, soapy water.

"Just rench'm out good with some cool water and dry'm quick so they'll stay cured," Miss Lena Pearl had instructed Beaufort Junior when he first started to help her. "If they's any germs left, they'll get cooked out. There ain't nothing worse than a uncured skillet for baking a pineapple upside-down cake."

If she was running behind sometimes she got Beaufort Junior to arrange the slices of pineapple in the bottom of the skillets with a half of a cherry in each pineapple hole.

"Be careful to put them cherries in upside-down so they'll be right-side-up when I turn cake upside-down."

Beaufort Junior got good at his job. Once when the cake lady was laid up for the better part of two weeks with the Asian flu that was going around that winter, Beaufort Junior took over the baking. Folks said from the taste of Beaufort Junior's cakes, pies, and rolls, they couldn't tell the cake lady herself had not baked 'em. When the cake lady heard of that reaction to Beaufort Junior's baking, she acted like she had her feelings hurt, but it was well known she was as proud as she could be of Beaufort Junior. She and Mr. Leonard had had no children of their own so Miss Lena Pearl kind of adopted Beaufort Junior, which worked out good for everybody since his own mama died of cancer when Beaufort Junior was no more than four or five years old.

"You did what!" Miss Lena Pearl exclaimed a second time before Beaufort Junior had a chance to answer her the first time.

"He was coming at me with a poker in his hand. I didn't know what to do so I picked up a flower pot and threw it at him."

"Was he drunk?"

"No, ma'am, I don't think so. You know Daddy don't drink. He was just mad, I guess. His face was all red, and he was cussin' like I never heard him cuss before. But, Miss Lena Pearl, I hope me die, I don't know what he was mad about. He whipped me a few times with his hand when I was little and once he used his belt, but he never used anything like a poker before. I swear before God."

"Ain't no need to swear before God nor nobody else."

Miss Lena Pearl reflected for a minute before she spoke further.

"Well, he's so hard-headed he probably ain't dead, but we better go see about him all the same."

Miss Lena Pearl told Beaufort Junior to back her black 1939 Ford out of the garage. She did not drive herself, but she kept the car when Mr. Leonard died so when she had to call on a neighbor to drive her to the doctor or something they wouldn't have to use up their gas.

"No need to do that," my mother said. "I'll drive you."

Miss Lena Pearl didn't bother to take off her white apron or the flowered scarf she kept tied around her head when she baked. Wisps of gray hair yet streaked with black came out around the edge of the flowered scarf. She wore no makeup to cover the age lines at the corners of her mouth. Her dark brown eyes danced with fear and excitement.

We all got in my mother's 1950 Chevrolet. Beaufort Junior and I sat in the back. He was tall and lanky with bright red hair. He sat leaned forward with his hands held palms together and tucked between his knees. Miss Lena Pearl sat in the front with my mother. My mother drove us the six or eight blocks that separate Miss Lena Pearl's house from the white clapboard three-room house in the mill village where Big Beaufort and Beaufort Junior lived.

When we got there, we found Chief Hugh Gatlin's black 1951 Ford parked in front of the house with the red light flashing on top. Some of the neighbors must have called him. Hugh Gatlin was standing on the front porch. He held his police hat in his hand, scratching his head like he didn't know what to do. Several neighbors had gathered in the yard. An awful fuss could be heard coming from inside the house.

It was unlike our chief of police to be perplexed. Customarily, he would know what needed to be done and move quickly to do it. This was different.

"Hugh Gatlin, what's going on here?" asked the cake lady as she marched up the stairs to the porch.

Beaufort Junior stayed back in the crowd with my mother and me. My mother reached down and put one hand on my shoulder. Shortly I saw her reach up and put her other hand on Beaufort Junior's shoulder. She had been his teacher when he was in sixth grade.

"Big Beaufort's done lost his mind, I guess," said the chief to the cake lady. "He's in there with a poker bustin' up all the dishes and the furniture. It ain't like him to act that way. It's like the devil or something's got in him. I've radioed the sheriff for some backup before I go in. The only way I could stop him by myself would be to hurt him real bad, and there ain't no need to do that. I just hope he don't hurt his own self while we're waitin'."

"Stand aside," said the cake lady.

"Hold on, Miss Lena Pearl," said the chief. "You ain't goin' in there."

"Hugh Gatlin," said the cake lady, "I've known you since the next day after you was born. I took a dozen yeast rolls to your mama and a plate of sliced ham to tell her how proud I was you was finally here after all the trouble you had caused her for nine long months. As I recall it, while I was there, you wet your pants, and I changed your dipper. There ain't no way you're going to tell me what to do nor when I can come and when I can go. It don't make no difference if you are the chief of police. Now stand aside."

Hugh Gatlin put his hat back on his head and stood aside.

Without the least hesitation, the cake lady opened the door and walked in the house. Big Beaufort was in the kitchen. As soon as cake lady walked in, whatever had gotten into Big Beaufort left him. Right off, the fuss stropped.

"My goodness, Beaufort," she said as she looked around, "just look what a mess you have made. What in the world's got you so upset?" She was speaking in a still, strong voice.

Big Beaufort let out a string of cuss words a mile long and said, "Don't you come in here with none of your sweet talk. This ain't none of your business."

"Now, Beaufort, you know I don't take to language like that, and of course this is my business. Anything's got you this upset is my business. What is it, son?"

"Don't you 'son' me. I know who you are."

"Of course you know who I am. I'm the cake lady, and I'll call you son anytime it pleases me to do so. Now let me see to that cut on your head."

She ran some water from the kitchen sink on to a paper towel and gently touched it to Big Beaufort's head.

"That ain't too bad. I think if I squeeze it together a little and put a Band-Aid on it to hold it closed, there won't be no need to get Dr. Leroy to put a stitch in it. Now, while I bandage up your head, you just tell the cake lady what hurt you so bad.

"Where's your first aid kit?"

"In the cabinet in the bathroom."

"You sit down there by the table while I get it, and for goodness' sakes put that poker down."

By that time, Beaufort Junior had made his way up to the porch and was standing just outside the door so he could hear. The others of us had gathered on the porch as well. My mother kept her hand on my shoulder as we made our way to the porch.

"My boy's one of them," we all heard Big Beaufort say.

"One of what?" asked the cake lady.

"One of them."

"One of what, Beaufort. I can't read your mind."

"You know, one of *them*. Frank Spivey come by here late this afternoon and said he didn't know how to tell me, and he said he had put it off as long as he could, but last Saturday afternoon when he was coming back from fishin' he seen Beaufort Junior and some man he didn't know down by the spillway, and they didn't have on no clothes."

"That don't mean nothing, Big Beaufort. Didn't you skinny-dip down by the spillway when you was a boy?"

"Well, sure I did, and that's just what I told Frank, but Frank said there was a lot more than skinny-dippin' goin' on. He said Beaufort Junior and the man he didn't know was havin' at each other like two bull minks."

When Beaufort Junior heard what his daddy said, he broke and ran through the crowd out in the direction of the woods that came up to the edge of the mill village.

A silence fell across the porch. Hugh Gatlin took his hat off and hung his head. I felt my mother squeeze my shoulder. After a minute or so, Hugh Gatlin turned to the people gathered there and said, "OK, folks, there ain't nothing else to be done here. You can all go on your way. Thank you for everything."

The crowd broke up and left. The silence continued until everyone but me and my mother were out of the yard.

"I'll stay and drive Lena Pearl home," said my mother.

"That'd be mighty nice of you," said the chief.

My mother and I sat in the swing on the porch while the cake lady bandaged Big Beaufort's head. My mother considered the ferns growing in pots and fingered the one closest to the swing.

"Beaufort's kept his wife's ferns healthy all these years." She said it more to herself than to me.

I studied the cake lady and Big Beaufort Johnson through the window.

"Mama, what's a bull mink?" I whispered.

"A mink is a soft furry animal. They make coats for rich women out of their skins."

"I know that much. Is a bull mink like a bull calf?"

"Yes."

Like all good teachers, she knew exactly when to end the lesson. The time would come for me to understand.

After Big Beaufort's head was tied up, my mother stuck her head in the door and offered to help clean up. The cake lady held up her hand so as to let my mother know she should stay on the porch. Leaving the mess as it was, the cake lady went into Big Beaufort's bedroom and turned down the covers on his bed.

"Beaufort," she said, "when you got on your pajamas come get me. I'll be in the kitchen."

Big Beaufort did as he was told.

"Now, Beaufort," the cake lady said when he had called her back into the room, "you kneel here with me beside the bed. We got some praying to do."

So it was that Big Beaufort Johnson, all six feet three inches and two hundred and fifty pounds of him, knelt with the cake lady beside his bed just like he was a little boy.

"Lord," prayed the cake lady out loud, "we don't understand these things, how it is Beaufort Junior nor anybody else would want to do what Frank Spivey says he seen him do; but we do know he is a good boy; and we know Big Beaufort has raised him right; and we know Big Beaufort loves his boy with a deep, deep love else he wouldn't have carried on like he did. We need you now, Lord. We need you to keep Beaufort Junior safe no matter where he is at, and we need something else just as much. We need you to cool the hot fire in this good man's soul. He's grieved enough now, and he needs a good night of rest. Give him rest, Lord. Give him rest. Give him rest in his body and give him rest in his mind. Amen."

With that Big Beaufort got in bed and the cake lady tucked him in like he might have been three or four years old.

"I'll come back in the morning to help you clean up this mess," she said as she turned out the light and moved toward the door. "Maybe I'll bring some hot rolls and country ham for breakfast.

"And one more thing," she said. "Why don't we leave the door un-locked just in case Beaufort Junior decides to come home."

"He's got a key," said the boy's father.

"He'd probably like it if he found the door unlocked if he comes home," said the cake lady. "I'll just leave it unlocked as I go out, if that's alright with you."

There was a pause. Then Big Beaufort said, "You can leave it unlocked."

Beaufort Junior didn't come home for two solid weeks, but when he got there, the door was unlocked.

three

You Give Them Something To Eat
(Mark 6:30–44)

(In the Context of Mark 6:4b–29)

Notes on the Text

IT CAN BE ARGUED that Mark's account of the feeding of the five thousand is *the* focal point of his gospel narrative and thus the focal point of the gospel's message to the church. That case could logically be based on Jesus' instruction to disciples (i.e., the church) for *them* (the church) to feed the hungry crowd (verse 37).[1] While I agree it is a crucially important text, I am not quite willing to give it superlative status among so many important texts deserving of the designation. That said, the story of the feeding of the five thousand does stand as a cornerstone of the ministry of Jesus. Indeed, the story was so important to the early church that it is among the few episodes (and only miracle story) included in all four of the New Testament gospels (Matt 14:13–21; Luke 9:10–17; John 6:1–15). Moreover, the story is so important to every generation of the church that readers should not get lost in concentrating solely on the role of Jesus as a miracle worker. In doing so they may neglect focusing on the deeper meanings of the text. For example, in Mark's version, with its companion piece, the feeding of the

1. While I do not know whether Robert Brawley would argue that this text is *the* focal point of Mark's gospel, I am deeply indebted to him for pointing me to its crucial importance. As further evidence of its importance Brawley notes that the episode takes place in a "deserted place," which is to say in a place apart from the all-pervasive power of the empire. Brawley's observations were made in critical notes on an early manuscript of this book.

four thousand (Mark 8:1–9), it forms brackets highlighting key themes in Jesus' ministry which are recounted between the brackets. That alone puts us on notice that there is much more in here than a simple miracle story. (See notes on the text in chapter 4 for more information on Mark's use of bracketing material.)

Apart from the obvious sacramental overtones and underpinnings of this important text, it has a number of salient silences. For our purposes we shall examine only two: 1) The intriguing proximity of the text to Mark's retrospective recounting of the beheading of Jesus' cousin, John the Baptist (Mark 6:14–29); and 2) Mark's silence on what Jesus had in mind when he told the disciples (the church) to feed the hungry crowd. To say only that they had five loaves and two fish is entirely too prosaic.

As to the former, the story of the beheading of John the Baptist has for centuries captured the imagination of the art world. One thinks immediately of the opera by Richard Strauss and the stage play by Oscar Wilde, both of whom give the dancing girl a name . . . Salome. There are many other artistic offerings of the episode, some famous and some not so famous. In Mark's initial telling of the story, however, it does nothing so much as stand as a stark interruption to his gospel narrative. The story line is developed like this: In his ministry on his home turf, Galilee, Jesus went to his hometown where he was rejected (Mark 6:1–6a). Jesus then sent the disciples out in pairs in what one assumes was a kind of test ministry wherein they preached, cast out demons (restored sanity?), and healed the sick (Mark 6:6b–13). When the disciples returned, one imagines exhausted from their labors, Jesus took them away, as it were, from the maddening crowd for a debriefing only to discover that the hungry crowd had beat them to their "deserted place."

That's the plot line. That is, it's the plot line except for the intrusion, seemingly from out of nowhere, of the dramatic account of the bloody execution of an itinerant preacher for the crime of speaking truth—truth that, by the way, posed a serious threat both to leaders of the synagogue and the empire. It is a captivating tale of all pervasive imperial power and greed gone mad in its treatment of seemingly powerless people. Underlying that is the conscious or unconscious complicity of the people of God in the exercise of imperial power. It is, to say the least, a captivating tale, but why drop it in the middle of the story of disciples learning how to be the church? Surely it was no accidental placement, but why here?

The stories that follow will attempt to provide possible answers to that question as well as to the related question of what, beyond five loaves and two fish, Jesus had in mind for disciples to give to the hungry crowd. The hope is that my stories will inspire readers or groups of readers to explore these as well as other options. As before, in the tradition of using midrash to interpret Scripture, in one of the stories I enter the text and add fictitious material. The other one, also fictitious, is set in my hometown. While the characters in the latter are composites, the issues they faced were and are real.

The Night Jesus Said, "Ah Ha"

The apostles gathered around Jesus, and told him all that they had done and taught. He said to them, "Come away to a deserted place all by yourselves and rest a while." For many were coming and going, and they had no leisure even to eat. And they went away in the boat to a deserted place by themselves. Now many saw them going and recognized them, and they hurried there on foot from all the towns and arrived ahead of them. As he went ashore, he saw a great crowd; and he had compassion for them, because they were like sheep without a shepherd; and he began to teach them many things. When it grew late, his disciples came to him and said, "This is a deserted place, and the hour is now very late; send them away so that they may go into the surrounding country and villages and buy some things for themselves to eat." But he answered them, "You give them something to eat." They said to him, "Are we to go and buy two hundred denarii worth of bread and give it to them to eat?" And he said to them, "How many loaves have you. Go and see." When they had found out, they said, "Five, and two fish." Then he ordered them to get all the people to sit down in groups on the green grass. So they sat down in groups of hundreds and of fifties. Taking the five loaves and the two fish, he looked up to heaven, and blessed and broke the loaves, and gave them to his disciples to set before the people; and he divided the two fish among them all. And all ate and were filled; and they took up twelve baskets full of broken pieces and of the fish. Those who had eaten the loaves numbered five thousand men.

By the time the crowds left, the day was far spent. Jesus and his disciples chose to stay in the deserted place for the night. When they had kindled a fire and filled themselves with leftover bread and fish, one of the disciples asked Jesus, "Tell me, Master, when you told us to give the crowd something to eat, what did you think *we* had to give them? You must have had more in mind than a paltry serving of five fish and two loaves of bread."

"Ah," said Jesus in a voice that said he understood the question but wasn't going to answer it. For disciples accustomed to making bumbling mistakes and being admonished for their silly misunderstandings, a simple *ah* seemed a good alternative.

Jesus then said to the disciples, "Tell me about your mission among the villages? How did it go?"

Two by two they began to tell their stories. Andrew told of embracing a widower crazy with grief and remorse. His wife had died giving birth to their first child. According to Andrew, the young man wept openly into his shoulder.

"Except for greeting friends, I've never embraced a man like that, and certainly not a stranger."

Andrew was known as a man's man.

"How did it make you feel," asked Jesus, "to have a man crazy with grief cry on your shoulder?"

Andrew reflected a moment then said too offhandedly, "It felt alright."

Jesus didn't say anything. He just looked at Andrew.

Andrew finally said, "It felt good."

"And how did it make the young man feel?"

"It seemed to make him feel better."

"Ah," said Jesus.

Two of them told of being asked, in no uncertain terms, to leave the synagogue because the priests said the Roman governor and his henchmen were coming for tea, only they didn't call his entourage henchmen.

"And how did that make you feel?" asked Jesus.

"Mad as hell," said Simon Peter.

Simon was never at a loss for words.

"You weren't even there," said James.

"I know," said Simon, "but it made me mad as hell when I heard about it."

"Ah," said Jesus.

Two told of visiting a man in jail. They heard about him through his wife who was begging bread on the streets to feed their children. His crime was not paying his taxes to Rome when actually, the woman explained, he had paid his taxes but had not been able to pay the bribe to the tax collector so the tax collector kept the taxes and listed him as delinquent.

When they had finished the story one of them added, "And would you believe the tax collector is a Jew. He's one of us."

"It's the way of it," said Matthew.

Matthew had once been a tax collector who had himself been too thick with the Roman army of occupation.

"Ah," said Jesus.

Two told of teaching children on the steps of the synagogue and of their parents who gathered around to listen. "That is, they listened until the priests chased us off," said John. "They told the children our teachings were nonsense, and then when we gathered again at the city gate, the soldiers made us move on."

"Ah," said Jesus.

On and on they went, two by two, telling of this healing and of that teaching and of another anointing and of the odd times they upset the Roman soldiers.

Finally Simon Peter said, "Strange, isn't it, how some of them love us and some of them hate us even when we tell all of them the same stories?"

"What's so strange about that?" said Judas. "Just look what came of the baptizer. John's disciples loved him, but when he spoke truth to the empire it got his head delivered up on a platter."

"Ah ha," said Jesus.

Then he added, "Now, what was your question about you feeding all those hungry people?"

The Truth What Needs To Be Spoke

When we were in the ninth grade in Great Falls High School, our English teacher, Miss Mary Jane Creighton, introduced us to English literature. Miss Mary Jane Creighton, though she was small of stature, was a powerful teacher. My friend and classmate, Ricky Joe Bradley, as strange as it sounds, got really turned on to the subject. That year he especially admired *Gulliver's Travels*. In the tenth grade, again under the strong and animated influence of Miss Mary Jane Creighton, Ricky Joe was mightily impressed with *Animal Farm*, and in eleventh grade he had the same response to *Lord of the Flies*. To hear Ricky Joe tell it, the world as seen by Jonathan Swift was not all that different from the world as he saw it right there in Great Falls, South Carolina. The same he found to be true of the world as seen by George Orwell and William Golding.

On the day Ricky Joe Bradley's mama died in the front room of their six-room mill house on Circle Street, Ricky Joe's daddy, Ozzie Bradley, took down his double-barrel shotgun, put a shell in each of the chambers, went out in the backyard, propped the butt of the shotgun against a limb in the mimosa tree he had planted many years before, put the muzzle in his mouth, and pulled both triggers at the same time. They say there wasn't enough of Ozzie Bradley's head left for Jack Hodge to put it back together. Jack Hodge was the embalmer at Hodge and Horton Funeral Home, one of the few businesses left in town.

Ricky Joe was my friend from childhood. Early on in summer and on Saturdays during the school year, we built forts in the woods behind my house, played rolly bat, shot baskets, and picked up games of football in his back yard. On rainy days we went inside and played checkers or Monopoly. Later, at considerable length, we pooled our considerable ignorance about girls, and we went skinny-dipping down by the spillway. By the time Ricky Joe's mama and daddy died, Ricky Joe was teaching high school English in North Charleston, South Carolina and I was preaching in Anniston, Alabama.

Ricky Joe called to tell me what had happened. A man of few words, he recounted the basics of how his mama had labored many years from breathing disorders brought on by thirty-five years of working in the cotton mills. It was not for nothing that shift workers in the cotton mills were known as lintheads. It was well known they could call each other by that name, but for anyone else to do so was fighting words. Ricky Joe went on to say how the last few months had been especially hard for his mama, and how when she died his daddy, like he had just been waiting for it to happen, went out in the backyard and shot himself.

After I had expressed my initial shock and grief, Ricky Joe said since his mama and daddy weren't churchgoing people and didn't have a preacher would I come home and conduct their funeral?

I told him I'd be honored to do so.

After I agreed, he told me the preacher from the Holiness Church had come by when he heard the news. Ricky Joe said he got the feeling the preacher came by because he wanted Ricky Joe to ask him to conduct the funeral just so he could tell everybody that since his daddy killed himself he was going to hell. Then Ricky Joe wanted to know if I believed that?

"Not for one minute," I said. "Beside his grief and the mills closing, I don't know what was troubling your daddy, but I do firmly believe your mama is breathing easy now, your daddy is at peace, and they are in the very place that was made for them since before the beginning of time."

All he could do was thank me through his tears before he had to hang up.

Ricky Joe was the youngest of the three children of Ozzie and Mamie Bradley. Theirs was not an easy life. Ozzie Junior, or "Junior" as he was known, got his legs blown off in Korea. The same injury left him impotent. He came home and lived off his disability check and pain pills. Eventually he drank himself to death. Ricky Joe's sister, Opel, got pregnant in the eleventh grade and dropped out of school. She married the boy who got her pregnant. Without a high school education, he was lucky to get a job as a sweeper in the mill. He moved in with the Bradleys, saying it would be for only a few months until they could get on their feet. They never got on their feet. The marriage didn't last much longer than it took the baby to be born. One day Opel's husband said he was going out to shoot some pool with his friends. He left home and never came back.

Ozzie and Mamie Bradley put all their hopes in Ricky Joe. As it happened, their hopes were well placed. By pooling their income and pinching every penny they could get their hands on, and with Ricky Joe getting a job washing dishes in the cafeteria, Ricky Joe Bradley, the first person in his family to do so, graduated from the University of South Carolina. He graduated with honors and with a double major in English and education. That's when he took a job teaching English in North Charleston, and that's when he changed his name from Ricky Joe to Richard.

He graduated just in time. As it happened, shortly after Ricky Joe . . . that is shortly after *Richard* . . . took his job in North Charleston, the decision was made at company headquarters in far off New York City that the mills in Great Falls, all three of them, would close. The town was distraught. Everywhere you turned, despair was so thick it was like you could cut it with a knife. There were three and even four generations of people who had known nothing but working in those mills.

Like almost everyone else in town, overnight Ozzie and Mamie Bradley were out of work. Soon after the mills closed, virtually every merchant in town was forced to go out of business. Those who were young enough went elsewhere to find jobs. Others, like Ozzie and Mamie, were too old to start over, too young to retire, and too proud to go on the dole.

Before the funeral, Ricky Joe and his sister had to rearrange the furniture in the front room to accommodate two caskets. After they had done that, they sprayed Lysol all around to get rid of the odor of sickness left by their mother in her final days. Jack Hodge was able to get Mamie Bradley's body fixed up real pretty for viewing. She had on her church clothes, not that she was much of a churchgoer. Still, except for her not breathing, from the looks of her, you wouldn't have thought she'd been sick a day in her life. That she looked so lifelike and healthy seemed a comfort to Ricky Joe and Opel.

They kept Ozzie's casket closed.

The funeral was held there in the living room. So the crowd that spilled out onto the front porch and into the yard could hear, they borrowed the sound system used by the Saturday Night Steppers for calling square dances. In the service, when it was Ricky Joe's turn to speak he showed no sign of bitterness. He spoke only of pride and gratitude for his parents. Like Ricky Joe, I said no unkind words. What I did and said was pretty much standard Presbyterian fare. As calmly and as strongly as I could, I claimed resurrection hope for both Mamie and Ozzie. I also said there was no need to feel like anybody had to make sense out of something that made no sense, and I did the best I could to give everybody permission to grieve as deeply as they needed to. Ricky Joe and Opel seemed satisfied. I left, however, with the uneasy feeling that something important had gone unsaid.

Still, all things considered, the services at home and at the cemetery had gone smoothly enough. It was a different matter altogether at the gathering that followed. Ricky Joe asked me to go with him to Mike Simpson's Sinclair Station down at the end of Dearborn Street. Beside the funeral home and a small grocery store, it was one of the few businesses in town that was still in operation. It was Mike's custom when one of his regulars died to close the doors of his station except to those he invited and to pass out ice cold Pabst Blue Ribbon beer. The beer on those occasions was on the house. He said it was better than spending a bunch of money on flowers or having his wife take a casserole to the house where they already had more food than they could eat in a month of Sundays.

When Mike handed me a beer and I took it, Clarence Muckenfus called out across the room, "Ain't never heard of a preacher what drinks beer."

"I try not to drink more than I figure Jesus drank, and that's the advice I give to everybody who drinks."

"How much do you figure he drank?"

"Well, there's no record he ever got drunk."

"I can't make no promise like that."

The exchange lightened the mood but not very much.

When everyone had a beer, Mike held his up and said, "Here's to our friend Ozzie and to his good wife Mamie."

"Here, here."

Then the stories started.

"I tell you one thing. That Ozzie and Mamie could flat out dance. I knowed'm back when they was sixteen and seventeen. They could flat-out 'nough cut a rug."

"Now that Ozzie, he loved to hunt. Couldn't hit the broad side of a barn, you understand, but that didn't slow him down none."

The mood was beginning to lighten a bit more.

"But, Lordy, how he could fish. He knowed where every bream bed in the river was to be found, and he could catch them suckers by the dozen . . . and I mean nice big 'uns . . . good eatin' size . . . like the size of your hand."

"But do you think he'd tell you where them bream beds was? Hell no. Or if he told you some place or other you could tell from the twinkle in his eye he was lyin.'"

Everybody laughed.

Then suddenly the mood changed. It was Danny Crinshaw's turn to speak. Danny was Ozzie's oldest and dearest friend. For many years they worked side by side and covered for each other in the card room of Number Two Mill.

Danny pulled his handkerchief out of the hip pocket of his overalls and blew his nose loudly. When he'd wiped his nose he said, "I tell you one goddamn thing, and I hope-me-die it's the truth if the truth was ever spoke.

"S'cuse my French, preacher, or maybe you try not to cuss no more than you figure Jesus cussed."

"I don't figure Jesus did a whole lot of cussing, but there is a record of him cursing a fig tree and there's no telling what words he used when he drove the money changers out of the temple; but I'm sure he said what needed to be said. You go right ahead, Mr. Crinshaw. Sounds to me like you're about to say what needs to be said."

"Well from all I hear Jesus went through, couldn't nobody blame him if he cussed a lot, but what I'm here to tell you is them goddamn bosses and their highfalutin' ways in New York City kilt Mamie and Ozzie Bradley just as shore as they woulda if they had'a broke in Mamie's room in the dark of night and held a piller over her face, or if they'd been in the yard with Ozzie and pulled them triggers. They think their shit don't stink, but I can tell you this much: if it don't it's because Ozzie and Mamie and the rest of us lintheads made them sorry-assed sons-a-bitches so rich they could buy as much Air Wick as it would take to cover it. All them years Mamie breathed all that cotton dust and do you think them tight-assed, neck-tied bosses in New York cared enough to put a decent exhaust fan anywhere in the whole goddamn mill? And that ain't all. That ain't near all. How about our so-called *friends*, the ones who kept their noses up the bosses' asses and got to be second hands? Do you think they ever once asked for a decent fan? Hell no.

"And there's one other damned thing. That Ozzie, he was one proud man . . . too proud really. He didn't want to ask for nothing even after the mills closed. About a month ago he come to me in the dark of night with his eyes red and head hung low. I ain't ever seen him lookin' like that, and he hadn't had a drop to drink either. He was wantin' to know if he could borrow enough to get a tank of oxygen for Mamie to help ease her breathin' because they was about out. It looked like he might fall over dead right there for having to ask so I told him, 'Hell no, he couldn't borrow a damn thing from me, but I'd give him anything I had if he needed it.' Then I told him I'd do such a thing only 'cause I knowed full well he'd do the same for me.

"After I told him that he eased off a bit, and I went in the house and got a hundred dollar bill from the coffee can where I keep my severance money.

I stuffed it in his overall pocket without him seeing how much it was and hoped it wouldn't make him feel too bad when he seen. Damn, that man was proud."

The room fell silent except for the sound of a beer opening. Danny wiped his eyes with the back of his hand. Mike handed him the beer he'd just opened.

"What do you think, preacher?" asked Mike. "Do you figure Jesus would drink as much as two beers if his best friend was so broke up and downhearted that he shot hisself?"

"I strongly suspect he would."

Ricky Joe put his hand on the shoulder of his daddy's old friend. He squeezed firmly and said, "Thank you, Mr. Crinshaw. You spoke the truth and you spoke it from the heart. I'm deeply grateful. I'll never forget what you said."

As beer bottles were drained the room began to empty. As each man left, he shook Ricky Joe's hand. More than one of them was careful to tell Ricky Joe how proud of him his mama and daddy had been. I heard several of them say Ricky Joe ought to come back to Great Falls and teach.

Later, as Ricky Joe was taking me back to Greenlawn Cemetery for me to get in my car and head back to Alabama, I said to him, "What about it? Why don't you come back to Great Falls and teach? More than ever the children left in town need somebody like Miss Mary Jane Creighton to help them catch a vision."

Without hesitating he said, not in an angry voice, "Why don't you come back to Great Falls and preach?"

four

The Second Touch
(Mark 8:22–26)

Notes on the Text

IN THIS STORY OF Jesus restoring sight to a blind person in Bethsaida, those seeking out silences in Mark will be tempted at first glance to notice Jesus' use of a salve made of his own saliva. It is true, of course, Mark provides no explanation for the use of such a practice. As it turns out, however, that was a common first-century home remedy. Jesus' followers and Mark's first readers would not have seen it as particularly unusual.[1] For purposes here, the more pressing questions is why it was necessary for the man to be touched twice before he could see clearly. While the immediate text offers no explanation, the larger context in which the story is set provides some clues. *Belief or Disbelief*

The story of the second touch is one of two stories of restored sight that form what is known in literary circles as an *inclusio*. The second is the story of the healing of Blind Bartimaeus in 10:46–52. Together the stories form something like brackets that hold the material between them together. Within the brackets the reader is put on notice to watch for signs of blindness that were in need of a healing touch, or dare we say it, signs of blurred vision that needed a second healing touch. Indeed, even a casual scan of the material between 8:22 and 10:52 shows that the disciples on several occasions just didn't understand what Jesus was teaching and doing or, at best, were unable to see clearly the hope that was with them in the person

---

1. Lamar Williamson, *Mark*, Interpretation (Atlanta: John Knox, 1983) 147.

of Jesus. For example, there was Peter's famous affirmation of faith in 8:29 in which Peter declared that Jesus is the Messiah. But then in the very next paragraph, it becomes clear Peter, at best, had only a clouded view of what that means. Then later in 9:9–13, of all things, there is an account of the disciples getting in an argument about which one of them was "greatest." On the heels of that gross misunderstanding there follows an account of the disciples' utter failure in their effort to bring healing to a poor demented boy. Jesus, as it were, had to clean up after them. And so it went. *true belief?*

More directly to Mark's point, readers of Mark should not forget, as has been pointed out in other chapters, it is widely recognized that where Mark used the word *disciples*, the word *church* can easily be substituted. That being so, could it be that, according to Mark, there is a kind of universal need for a second touch in the church since the church is seldom able to see clearly the hope contained in the gospel we profess and the redemption that is at hand?

The tales that follow are an effort to bring into focus the need for a second healing touch among the faithful. Once again, in the first two tales I enter the text and add playful and entirely fictitious details. The third and fourth are fictionalized short stories drawn from experiences in my childhood and youth, respectively.

48 passages Re/the Messianic Secret

1. not just about healing
2. True that ministry was ultimately about dying & Ressurection
3. Surprise of the 2nd Touch

The Noirekins

[Jesus and his disciples] came to Bethsaida. Some people brought a blind man to him and begged him to touch him. He took the blind man by the hand and led him out of the village; and when he had put saliva on his eyes and laid his hands on him, he asked him, "Can you see anything?"

Then, in less time than it takes a hummingbird to flap her wings or a gnat to wiggle his toes, there came, as if at once from nowhere and everywhere, four noirekins to sit on the blind man's shoulders, two on each side. Noirekins are tiny spirit creatures from the powers of darkness grim. As such, they are not constrained at all by such dimensions as time and space. They can enter and leave either or both at will. Noirekins have pointy features, dress in black, and have high squeaky voices.

The first noirekin leaned forward and whispered in the blind man's right ear. "Ah, Mr. Blind Man," said the first noirekin, "now that you can see, tell me what you see."

"I see money changers," said the blind man. "Big, fat money changers seated at their desks in glass cages across a busy street from the temple where hungry children are standing in line at the door holding out empty bowls."

"Yes," said the first noirekin in his high squeaky voice. "That's the way it is. The only hope is for the money changers' money to trickle down to the hungry. It's not a pretty sight. Perhaps . . . just perhaps, you would rather remain blind. The choice is yours. Hee, hee, hee," cackled the first noirekin in his high squeaky voice.

"I see," said the blind man, "but everything looks ugly."

The second noirekin leaned forward and whispered in the blind man's ear. "Ah, Mr. Blind Man," said the second noirekin, "now that you can see, tell me what you see."

"I see a great sea of garbage," said the blind man, "with mountainous waves of rubbish with a horde of people picking through it."

"Yes," said the second noirekin in her high squeaky voice, "that's the way it is. The only hope is for you to build a mansion high on a hill and leave the others to pick through your garbage, or perhaps . . . just perhaps, you would rather remain blind. The choice is yours, hee, hee, hee," cackled the second noirekin.

"I see," said the blind man, "but everything looks distorted."

The third noirekin, having shoved the first noirekin off the blind man's shoulder, took her place to whisper in the blind man's ear. "Ah, Mr. Blind Man, now that you can see, tell me what you see."

"I see a multitude of senators, governors, presidents, and kings. They are all talking at once and seem quite angry and no one is listening to anyone else."

"And that's the way it is," said the third noirekin. "The only hope is for you to have a tea party, or perhaps . . . just perhaps, you would rather remain blind. The choice is yours. Hee, hee, hee," cackled the third noirekin who almost fell from the blind man's shoulders she was laughing so hard.

"I see," said the blind man, "but everything looks ever so . . . unfair."

The fourth noirekin, kicked the second noirekin so hard it sent her off rubbing her shin, then whispered the fourth noirekin in the blind man's ear, "Ah, Mr. Blind Man, now that you can see, tell me what you see."

"I see a teeny council of holy people dressed in black robes, white albs, and brightly colored vestments of every kind; and, like the senators, governors, presidents, and kings, they are shouting at each other; only, unlike the senators, governors, presidents and kings, a few have gathered in the corners with their lips poked out. They seem to be pouting."

"Oh," said the fourth noirekin who was already laughing under his breath. "And what might they be arguing about?"

"They're arguing about who's greatest . . . no, wait, they're arguing about who's going to be in charge . . . no, wait, they're arguing about who can be in and who must stay out . . . no, they're arguing about who does what to whom in bed."

"And that's the way it is," said the fourth noirekin. "The only hope for the holy people is for them to divide into groups and go their separate ways, or perhaps . . . just perhaps, you would rather remain blind. The choice is yours. Hee, hee, hee," cackled the fourth noirekin who could no longer contain his enthusiasm.

"I see," said the blind man, "but everything looks twisted."

Then, in less time than it takes a hummingbird to flap her wings or a gnat to wiggle his toes, the noirekins were gone, and the blind man heard Jesus ask,

> "Can you see anything?"
> And the man looked up and said, "I can see people, but they look like trees, walking." Then Jesus laid his hands on his eyes again; and he looked intently and his sight was restored . . . and

> he saw everything clearly. Then [Jesus] sent him away to his home saying, "Do not even go into the village."

Tell no one what you see until the dawn of Easter.

I Understand Blindness

[Jesus and his disciples] came to Bethsaida. Some people brought a blind man to him and begged him to touch him. He took the blind man by the hand and led him out of the village; and when he had put saliva on his eyes and laid his hands on him . . .

Jesus then placed the blind man's hand on the shoulder of Andrew, one of the twelve, and told Andrew to lead the blind man to the stream a short distance away and to wash the saliva from the blind man's eyes.

Andrew did as Jesus asked.

When they had reached the stream, Andrew took a towel, dipped it in the cool water, and used it to bathe the blind man's eyes.

"What do you see?" Andrew asked the blind man.

"I see you," said the blind man, "but you look like . . . well, you look like a tree."

"A tree?" said Andrew. "I may be tall and skinny, but I'm no tree. Let's go and have Jesus touch you again."

"No, wait," said the blind man. "This is good enough."

"Good enough?" said Andrew. "Seeing people and they look like trees is not good enough . . . at least not to my way of thinking."

"I see everything I want to see," said the blind man with a little edge in his voice.

"What does that mean?"

"It means I can see enough not to step in cow dung." The edge in his voice had begun to sound as though it had a bitter taste.

"I don't understand."

"No, I expect you don't understand. People who can see don't always see. I understand blindness, and blindness understands me."

"I'm confused. Tell me more."

"Alright, I will," said the blind man. "If you must know, now, as it is, when I wake in the night and feel my wife's soft skin and smell the eucalyptus in her hair, I imagine her to be the most beautiful woman in the world. If I could see her as she really is, I might discover she is not as beautiful as I imagine."

"But you may find out she's even more beautiful than you think."

"Impossible," said the blind man. "It's not possible to be more beautiful than I think my wife is, but that's not all. From the place in the market where I beg, I can hear the Roman soldiers passing by and cursing;

sometimes I hear the screams of some poor wretches as the soldiers whip them with a cat-o'-nine-tails. I'd rather not see that.

"And that's still not all . . . not nearly all." The clip of the blind man's speech was picking up. "When I smell a rose it seems so sweet and beautiful, but then I feel its thorns and it seems mean and deceitful. I don't want to see that. When I hear my two children laugh and play I wish I could see them, but then I hear them fighting and crying. Who wants to see that?

"I can go on," said the blind man.

"Please do," said Andrew.

"OK, I will. On cold mornings when I milk the cow, I lean over and warm my ears, first one and then the other, on her warm belly, and I taste a dipper of her warm, sweet milk fresh from her udder. It gets my day off to a perfect start. Now I can see enough not to step in her dung, and that's good enough for me."

"Tell me," said Andrew, "do you see the children over there playing in the water?"

"Yes."

"How many are there?"

"Five."

"Are they safe?"

"How would I know?"

When Andrew had brought the blind man back to Jesus,

> [Jesus] asked him, "Can you see anything?"
> And the man looked up and said, "I can see people, but they look like trees, walking." Then Jesus laid his hands on his eyes again; and he looked intently and his sight was restored and he saw everything clearly. Then [Jesus] sent him away to his home saying, "Do not even go into the village."

The Long Road Home

The old man touched my mother's arm. Instinctively she jerked it back in the car. Penny, our Shetland sheepdog, went on full alert. His ears perked up, his eyes opened wide, and he growled softly. Mom's arm had been resting in the window of our 1941 Plymouth sedan. For long road trips Penny rode in the front seat with Mom. My brother Sparky and I rode in the backseat. Our father, known by us and by the men in his command as "Pappy," always traveled cross-country in convoy with his company. This time though he and the company had deployed to an undisclosed location in the European Theater. I was four years old at the time. Sparky is three years older. We had stopped at a country store to ask directions to the nearest tourist court, as they were known at the time. It was long before the days of modern motels.

The old man didn't notice my mother's reaction to his touch, or if he did, he didn't let on.

"Don't you worry about a thing, little lady," he said. "It's after five o'clock, and, what with rationing and all that, I ain't supposed to sell you no gas after five, but I don't see no harm in it. Besides, there ain't no tourist court this side of Chattanooga, at least not one fit for a lady like you and them two fine boys. My guess is you'll be needin' some gas to get you that far. It's for sure there ain't nobody else in these hills will sell you a drop of gas after five."

The old man retreated into the store to get the key to the gas pump. He was dressed in bib overalls over a starched white shirt buttoned to the neck.

Sparky and I had been well prepared for the trip.

"What's the first thing you do when you change a tire?" Pappy had asked, and he pointed to me.

"You ask Mama if she's got everything inside the car set just right," I answered by rote.

"Right. What's the second thing?" He pointed to Sparky.

"You get the 4 x 6 wedge out of the trunk and put it under the opposite tire on the down-hill side,"

I can't be sure whether I remember such lessons or remember being told about them. The story of my brother and me learning to change a tire runs deep in our family's lore. With many other such stories, it was told and retold at family gatherings and well embellished from time to time along the way. No matter. At its heart, the important truth of the story remains, and beside that, when called on to do so, I can yet change a tire. More than that, I yet treasure being trusted with such valuable information in time of crisis. Along with collecting tin cans and tin foil, it was our part in the war effort.

So the oft repeated lesson went. Pappy was getting us ready for the long trip home. When I think back on it, my mother, one of the most universally capable people of any gender I have ever known, could surely have changed a tire with one hand tied behind her back. Nevertheless, teaching his sons to change a tire was important to Pappy. In his mind, if not in reality, it was a way he could care for his family *in absentia*.

We were living in Henderson, Kentucky near his last duty station before he and his company were shipped out. Every morning when he left for work, for security reasons, we neither knew whether he would return at the end of the day nor where he would be going on the day he didn't come home. The plan was, on the day after he didn't come home, we would load up the Plymouth and drive to our hometown, Great Falls, South Carolina, to be near family. That's why it was important to Pappy for Sparky and me to know how to change a tire.

I don't remember much about living in Henderson. Like not being sure whether I remember the tire-changing lessons or remember hearing the story of it, I can't be sure I remember long Saturdays in a park by a river with Pappy, Mom, Sparky, and Penny. Maybe I've manufactured those Saturdays in my mind from the single picture we have of the four of us with our copper-colored dog in a park with a river in the background. In the picture I'm on Pappy's shoulders, Mom's hand is hooked over Pappy's arm, and Sparky is holding her other hand. Penny is standing faithfully beside Sparky. *Henderson, Kentucky, 1943* is written in pencil on the back. The day of the photo was cold. The trees were bare, we were bundled in winter coats, the sky was gray. Mom and Pappy are nestled against each other. As we looked into the camera, being held, no doubt, by a friendly stranger pressed into service, Sparky and I look nothing so much as safe. Our parents, though smiling a little, must have been nothing so much as frightened.

And, of course, one night Pappy didn't come home. We had been cautioned it would happen. They had even explained as best they could why it would happen. I suppose children can understand war about as well as anyone can understand something so utterly incomprehensible. With the table set and supper ready to put on the table, he didn't come home. At first Mom said maybe he was just running late and we would wait supper. Then she said we would eat and she would leave a plate in the oven to stay warm for him. Finally she put us both in the legged tub for what was to be the last time. When we had said our prayers and she had tucked us in bed, she said we would be leaving first thing in the morning for Great Falls. The first words she spoke confirming her sure knowledge that Pappy wasn't coming home was a prayer for his safety.

All these years later, I still can't imagine the anguish she must have felt.

The next day, she woke Sparky and me before the sun was up. I suspect she had not slept. Our clothes were laid out. Everything else was packed and ready to load in the car. The refrigerator had been emptied except for the milk to go on our Wheaties. The whole house had been cleaned.

After we had eaten breakfast, Mom washed and dried the dishes. As the sun was coming up, Sparky and I did all we could to help her get things loaded in the Plymouth. She locked the house, took the key to the landlady next door, hugged her, and thanked her for her war-time hospitality as she held out the cash to pay the last of the rent. The landlady, without comment, gently pressed the bills back in her hand.

It's a long way from Henderson, Kentucky to Great Falls, South Carolina. There were many mountains to cross, and of course Dwight David Eisenhower was yet fighting a war and had, at most, only begun to dream of his network of interstate highways. The route had been determined and carefully marked on a map. Other plans for travel had also been worked out long before. Because Pappy was in the army, we had an "A" ration sticker stuck to our windshield that meant we had enough ration stamps to buy gasoline for the trip. The tricky part was to find a filling station, as they were known then, before five o'clock.

I can recall little of the trip and most of what I think I might remember could easily be confused with other such long road trips with Sparky and me in the backseat and Mom and Penny in the front. I remember one tourist court where the cottages were shaped like tepees, another where the cottages were log cabins, and another where the cottages were white clabbered and tucked under huge shade trees. That one had a swing in the yard. The three of us sat in it while Mom read Uncle Remus stories to us. Once we spent the night in the upstairs of a large house. That time Sparky and I had to be especially quiet as Mom had promised the people who lived there we would. They did not usually allow children in their guest rooms.

That's surely more nights than we had to spend getting from Henderson, Kentucky to Great Falls, South Carolina. All of those memories couldn't possibly be from that trip, but I do remember the night we spent over a country store. I no longer know exactly where it was except that it was in the mountains with many switchback roads. It could have been in West Virginia or Tennessee.

For many miles Mom had been entertaining Sparky and me by having us see which one could be the first to spot a tourist court. All the while we could tell she was nervously looking at her watch and glancing down at the gasoline gauge.

Finally we came to the unpainted country store where the old man touched my mother's arm. It had rusting tin signs nailed to the wall advertising everything from animal feed to chewing tobacco. The porch had an old church pew against the wall and a checkerboard on a nail keg. On the edge of the porch was a gas pump with a long handle on one side and a glass container on top with gallons marked on the glass. Living quarters were above the store and extended over the porch. It was the stuff of a Norman Rockwell painting.

When the old man went back into the store to get the key to the gas pump the screen door slammed behind him. Years later, my mother said she would have left right then if she hadn't been desperate for gasoline. She spent the rest of her life grateful that she didn't leave.

Within minutes of the screen door slamming behind the old man it swung open again. That time it opened with purpose and determination. Out strode an old woman. She was tall and thin. Her long gray hair was platted and twisted in a bun on the back of her head. She was dressed in a flower-print dress over which she wore a white butcher's apron. Her pink sweater, like her husband's white shirt, was modestly buttoned at the neck. She took long deliberate strides across the porch, down the steps, and over to our car.

"Lord, honey," the woman said in her mountain twang. "I don't know where that man of mine went and put his manners. When he come in the store and told me what you wanted, the first thing I said to him was, 'Gas? That woman and them little boys don't need no gas. What they'll be needin' is a safe place spend the night. What was you going to do,' I said to him, 'just put some gas in that Plymouth and send her off twistin' around the mountain in the dark'a night?'

"That's what I said to him, and then I sent him off to catch us up a fryin' size chicken. Now you just get yourself out of that car. I bet you been drivin' all day and you must be wore slap out."

As we got out of the car the old woman said, "My man told me you'uns got a A sticker on your car. That can't mean but one thing. Like us, you got folks of fightin' the war. Our boy's over in North Africa drivin' a tank for General George S. Patton.

"Where's your man?"

"We don't know exactly," my mother said. "All we know is that he's on his way to some place in Europe."

That night we ate supper in their kitchen. Before supper, the store-keeper said, "I don't know about you'ens, but we're a prayin family."

"So are we," my mother assured him.

With the sacramental smell of fried chicken, cornbread, and green beans cooked in fatback on the table before us and the promise of an apple pie on the kitchen counter, the old man prayed. After thanking God for the bounty, he called his son by name and asked God to bring him and General George S. Patton home safely. Then he prayed, "Lord, you've brought strangers to be in our home this night. Bless this good woman and her boys. Go with them to their journey's end and bring her man home unharmed."

His prayers for us and for our father were heeded.

I can't recall now how the room where we slept looked. I do remember that the three of us plus Penny slept in the same room, and I remember the sheets smelled fresh like mountain air, and I remember the quilts on which my mother had commented favorably to our hostess were comfortable and made me feel safe.

The next morning, Mom paid for the gas. She knew better than to insist when there was no charge for the hospitality. As we were about to drive away, when the gentleman patted my mother on the arm, she neither recoiled nor did Penny growl. Rather she patted his hand in return as Penny settled himself beside her on the front seat, and Sparky and I claimed our respective sides of the backseat.

The Touch of Miss Mary Jane Creighton

When Miss Mary Jane Creighton touched Johnny Ray Mayfield on the shoulder and asked him a question, it was hard to tell whether Johnny Ray fell or dove out of his desk. Either way, Johnny Ray wound up on the floor in a pile of books and pencils with his desk on its side. Johnny Ray was not accustomed to being touched. Neither was he accustomed to being asked a question by a teacher . . . especially by one as young and pretty as Miss Mary Jane Creighton.

L coming as it does in the alphabet just before M meant that for those classes where the teachers in our high school had their students sit in alphabetical order I always sat just in front of Johnny Ray Mayfield. That is, I sat in front of Johnny Ray except in Miss Mary Jane Creighton's tenth-grade English class. Rather than front to back, Miss Creighton seated her class in alphabetical order from her left to her right as she faced the class. "I want you to know I'm reading you like a book," she said smiling all the while. I suppose she was establishing her position of authority. Establishing her authority wouldn't have been an easy task for a first-year teacher fresh out of college if Miss Mary Jane Creighton hadn't been so pretty, especially since she was shorter than most of us and probably weighed less than a hundred pounds. She wasn't exactly what you would call movie-star pretty. It was more like she was clean and wore clothes that always matched. Her dark brown hair was never out of place and her fingernails were neat. Strange how I remember her hands. If I were an artist, I think I could draw her hands from the picture that's yet in my mind . . . smooth palms, short fingers, rounded unpainted nails.

That she was reading us like a book is why, on a certain hot day in May of 1956, rather than sitting in front of Johnny Ray I was sitting beside him. It was not a good place to be: teeth green at the gums, dirty shirt too small, dirty dungarees too large, scuffed shoes, no socks, and thick hair, black as coal, greasy and uncombed. To top it all off he must not have been listening in the seventh grade when in health class our teacher told us it was time we should start using underarm deodorant.

There was a lot of talk at the Sanitary Barber Shop about Johnny Ray's mother, Mae Mayfield. When I was barely old enough to have any understanding of what he was saying, I heard Alford Brakefield, purveyor of town "news" who worked behind the first chair, say something like, "Ain't that Mae Mayfield something? Works the second shift at Number Two Mill, gets off at 12:00 then goes to Moe's mighty near every night and drinks beer just about 'til sunup. The way I hear it, she goes out back of Moe's most every night with a different man. What's she got? Four or five head of younguns? Guess she just leaves'm there to raise they own self, and, if you care to notice, ain't no two of them kids looks anything alike."

If it hadn't been for the reputation of Johnny Ray Mayfield's mother and for the way Johnny Ray smelled, nobody would have ever noticed him. The teachers didn't even notice him much. As strange as it sounds, the teachers didn't seem to mind that all Johnny Ray ever did in class was to sit and read one book or another he had checked out of the library. It didn't matter whether the class was math, history, biology, or English, everyday, all class long, Johnny Ray read.

On the day Miss Mary Jane Creighton called on Johnny Ray Mayfield and touched him on the shoulder, it was just before school was to be out for the summer. Exams were over, the grades had already been turned in to the office, and everybody was just counting down the minutes to three months of freedom. Never one to miss a teaching moment though, Miss Creighton used the time to review some rules of grammar. She was walking up and down the aisles between the desks and making up sentences. In each sentence she would deliberately make a grammatical error. For example, she would say something like *Bill and Joe was going to the store* or *Drive slow* or *The presents are for Sue and I.* Those were the easy ones. Sometimes they were harder or maybe even tricky. One of her favorites was *The rule is to never split an infinitive.*

Easy or tricky, after each sentence she would call a student's name and ask the student to correct the sentence. When she got to Johnny Ray she gave him an easy one, but since she just happened to be standing right beside him at the time she called on him she touched him on the shoulder when she called his name. That's when he fell into the aisle and sent books and pencils flying. Or maybe he dove. It was hard to tell.

Well, I want you to know Miss Mary Jane Crighton didn't bat an eye or break her stride. She just went on with the exercise like nothing unusual had happened. She called on the next student and asked her to help Johnny Ray with the sentence. Meanwhile, Johnny Ray picked himself up, gathered his books, and sat back down. If our teacher heard our snickers she didn't let on.

The exercise went on for awhile longer as Miss Creighton paced the aisles between the desks making up sentences as she went. The next time she got to Johnny Ray's desk she stopped, touched him on the shoulder again and said, "Johnny Ray, why don't you tell the class what you're reading." I can see her hand on his shoulder now. It was shaking just a little.

Johnny Ray didn't move a muscle except for the ones it took to move his mouth just enough to say, "*War and Peace*." He said it in such a low voice if I hadn't been seated right next to him I likely wouldn't have heard him.

"Ah, that's wonderful, Johnny Ray. Tell the class who wrote *War and Peace*." She kept her hand on his shoulder. He didn't move.

"Leo Tolstoy." Again Johnny Ray's voice was so low nobody but those right next to him could hear.

"That's right," said Miss Creighton. "Leo Tolstoy. *War and Peace* is one of my favorite novels," she said. "In fact, I like it so much I've read it twice."

"Three times. This makes four," said Johnny Ray.

"Four times! Wow! Tell the class what it's about."

"Russians."

"Well, yes, but what else?" There was a slight pause.

"Good and evil." There was another slight pause.

"You know, Johnny Ray, I think you nailed it.

"OK, class I have one more incorrect sentence for you before the bell rings.

> The red and the black, the red and the black,
> What do they lack, what do they lack?
> Nothing at all, nothing at all,
> The Great Falls Red Devils has it all."

It was a well-known cheer repeated many times at every football and basketball game, but before she could call on anyone the bell rang.

"OK, everybody think about that one until tomorrow," she said as we all headed for the door. She barely managed to add, "That's a tricky one."

If I hadn't been seated beside Johnny Ray Mayfield I wouldn't have heard him say as we stood up to leave, "'The Great Falls Red Devils *have* it all' unless you think of Red Devils collectively. Then *has* is correct."

five

The Naked Truth (Mark 14:51–52)
(In the Context of Mark 14:43–58)

Notes on the Text

THERE HAS BEEN MUCH ink spilled by scholars and others interested in the New Testament in the process of trying to determine exactly who wrote the Gospel of Mark. The truth is, no one knows, and barring the discovery of new information, no one is apt to figure it out with any degree of certainty. Of course, in the overall scheme of things, it doesn't make a particle of difference who wrote Mark, but it can be fun to speculate, and there have been set forth a number of intriguing theories. One of my favorite suggestions is that Mark was either written by Simon Peter or someone quite close to Simon Peter.

Another of my favorite suggestions is that this no-name naked young man who makes a cameo appearance in Mark's passion narrative is none other than Mark, and it is he who wrote the book that bears his name. No one knows, but I like the thought.

Except to say interpreters don't have a clue what these two verses mean or what their significance might be, commentaries are strangely and nearly completely silent on them. The verses seem to have been dropped in from nowhere. They certainly don't advance the plot in any significant way. Nevertheless, I am convinced Mark, who ever he (or she?) might have been, did not put the verses there by accident.

Could it be that the passion of our Lord exposes the naked truth of widespread complicity in the death of Jesus?

The tales that follow explore that possibility. As has been the pattern thus far, in the first two stories, in the tradition of midrash scholarship, I enter the biblical narrative and add fictitious details setting forth what I believe to be fanciful alternatives. The other tales, once again, are from my childhood and youth. Perhaps in them it can be seen why many have drawn the theological conclusion that complicity in the death of Jesus is virtually universal.

The Writer

Immediately, while [Jesus] was still speaking [to disciples], Judas, one of the twelve, arrived; and with him a crowd with swords and clubs, from the chief priests and the scribes and the elders.

Now the betrayer had given them a sign, saying, "The one I shall kiss is the man; arrest him and lead him away under guard."

So when he came, he went up to at once, and said, "Rabbi!" and he kissed him.

Then they laid hands on him and arrested him.

But one of those who stood near drew his sword and struck the slave of the high priest, cutting off his ear.

Then Jesus said to them, "Have you come out with swords and clubs to arrest me? Day after day I was with you in the temple teaching and you did not arrest me. But let the scriptures be fulfilled."

All of them deserted him and fled.

A certain young man was following him, wearing nothing but a linen cloth. They caught hold of him, but he left the linen cloth and ran off naked.

Startled and afraid, the young man pushed his way through the crowd and hid himself among the shrubs that bordered the ancient olive orchards of Gethsemane.

When the crowd moved away following the guards toward the home of the chief priest, the young man first tried to find his linen cloth. It was hopeless. He then made his way through the shadows of the orchard, ducking first behind one of the gnarled trees and then behind another. He didn't know where he was going or what he was going to do.

At last, trembling with fear and chill, he saw a small hovel on the edge of the orchard. A faint light was shining in the opening that served as its only window. The young man quietly made his way to the shack and crouched beneath the window. Slowly he raised his head just enough to peak through the opening.

Inside he saw an old man seated on a stool squinting to read a scroll by the faint light of a single oil lamp. The young man recognized the old man as someone often seen at temple. His name was Simeon.

Now it was Simeon who had been in the temple when Joseph and Mary brought Jesus there to fulfill the law soon after Jesus was born. Simeon was the one who had taken Jesus in his arms, recognized him as the Messiah. That is, Simeon recognized Jesus as the one on whom they had long waited. When he had said these things to Mary and Joseph, Simeon blessed the child. After he blessed Jesus, Simeon said to Mary, the mother of Jesus, "This child is destined for the falling and the rising of many in Israel, and to be a sign that will be opposed so that the inner thoughts of many will be revealed—and a sword will pierce your own soul too."[1]

Not knowing what else to do, the young man knocked at the door of the hovel and called out in a loud whisper, "Simeon, this is Writer. Remember me? I work in the temple assisting the high priests.

"I need your help."

Simeon opened the door slowly, held the light, squinted a bit, and finally spoke. "Yes," he said, "I do remember you. You're the young man who takes the lambs we bring at the time of making sacrifice. Do you always go about at night with no clothes?"

"No," said the young man. "Never before tonight, which is why I have come to you. I need your help," he said covering his nakedness as best he could with his hands. "Do you have a cloak I can borrow until I can go quickly to my room at the temple and get something of my own to put on? My linen cloth was pulled off by someone in the crowd when they arrested the man Jesus."

"So they arrested him," said Simeon. "It is as I feared."

He then eyed the young man named Writer from head to toe.

"Yes, of course," the old man went on. "Come in. Sit there on the stool while I see what I can find."

The young man sat, crossed his legs, and hunched over trying in every way he could to hide his nakedness.

"Let's see," said the old man as he plundered through some sacks pretending to search for a cloak. "What did you say your name is?"

"My name is Writer."

"What an unusual name."

"Yes, my mother dreamed I would learn to read and write. That's why she gave me over to work for the high priests. She left me with them soon after I was weaned.

"Have you found a cloak? Anything will do." Writer was feeling very much exposed.

"Not yet," said the old man, "but I'm sure I must have something. Let's see. That's far too big. This is soiled. This is too worn."

---

1. See Luke 2:34–45.

"Please hurry, sir. They are taking the man to the home of the chief priest. I'm sure they will soon be very busy and will want me to be there to go get this and go fetch that."

"Alright, I'll hurry," said the old man as he continued to riffle through old rags, "but first you must tell me the truth. What do you do with the unblemished lambs we give you for the sacrifice; and may I point out, sitting there in your present state is not a good time to be less than truthful?"

"If you must know," the young man said more sadly than with anger, "I sell them at market, buy sickly lambs at a much cheaper price, and return the profit to the priests' treasurer."

"Just as I suspected," said Simeon. "I may be old, but I'm not stupid. We take in beautiful lambs to be sacrificed and by the time of the ritual . . . well, you know. All these years I've just told myself God knows what's in my heart when I bring the unblemished lamb.

"What else do you do for the priests?" Simeon asked.

"Sweep up and things like that."

"Is that all?"

"Well, no. Sometimes when they have drunk much wine," he sounded disgusted, "they send me to get young girls for them."

"Ah," said the old man.

"I'm not proud of what I do," said Writer, still with sadness but also with an edge in his voice.

"Ah," said the old man a second time and waited. By then, he had even quit pretending to look for a cloak. He just leaned against the wall and looked at the young man with his legs crossed, one hand over his groin and the other across his chest.

"But tonight," the young man went on, "it became too much." Tears were welling in his eyes.

"And what happened tonight?" Simeon asked.

"Tonight one of the followers of Jesus, the one they call Judas, came to the priests and offered to betray Jesus for a price."

"Yes, go on."

"After a lot of haggling, they must have settled on thirty pieces of silver. That's how much they sent me to get from the treasury."

"And did you go get it?"

"Yes," said the young man. Abruptly he stood, no longer attempting to hide his nakedness.

"Those old fools!" the young man went on. "Damn them. Their only fear is that this man Jesus will expose them for the frauds they are."

"Expose them?" asked Simeon.

Writer, standing there naked before the old man, understood the irony in what he had just said. Instantly, his hand reached to cover his nakedness before he went on. "As soon as the guards left with Judas I realized what they were going to do at the behest of the priests and elders. The man Jesus has done nothing but good which is, of course, a threat to the priests, not to mention their cronies in the palace. I knew he must be warned so I ran from the house with nothing on but my linen cloth. There was no time to find my cloak. Desperately, I tried to find Jesus; but, since I knew no more than the guards as to where he was, all I could do was follow them at a distance and try to find an opportunity to get to Jesus before they did."

"Then what happened?"

"I got to Jesus too late. Just as I reached him, the deed was being carried out, and, do you know, the deed was done with a kiss."

After a pause, Simeon asked, "And then?"

"There was much confusion and shouting. Someone, one of Jesus' followers, drew a sword, and I think one of the guards was hurt, but I was too far back to see.

"Then as they were taking Jesus away, I think he actually looked in my direction. Yes, I'm certain he saw me in the crowd. I reached out and tried to help, but it was too late. It was just then that someone grabbed my linen cloth. I guess they were trying to stop me. No matter. My linen cloth came off, and you know the rest."

The two men, one very old and stooped beneath time and circumstance, the other young and exposed, stood looking at each other for several long seconds filled with nothing so much as silence. Finally the old man took off his cloak, handed it to the young man and said, "You must go now. Go to the house of the chief priest. I dare say you know your way around it. Because you're there so often, no one will be suspicious when you go to where they are keeping the prisoner. You may be the only one who can go to the man Jesus and see what you can do to make him more comfortable."

It was as though someone lit a candle in Writer's head. He wrapped the old man's cloak around him and bounded toward door of Simeon's hovel, but, before he left, Writer stopped in his tracks and turned to embrace the old man.

During the time Writer was with Simeon,

> They took Jesus to the high priest; and all the chief priests, the elders and the scribes were assembled. Peter followed him at a distance right into the court yard of the high priest; and he was sitting with the guards, warming himself at the fire.

Writer noticed Peter as he passed but said nothing.

When Writer got to the home of the high priest, he saw the great crowd standing outside. Deliberately, Writer made his way to the well and drew water to fill a jar; without saying anything to anyone along the way, he went to the place they kept prisoners.

When he got there, Writer said to the jailer, "The chief priest, as an act of kindness, has sent me with water for the prisoner."

"Kindness, indeed," shrugged the jailer, but he opened the door to the prisoner's cell.

"Jesus," said Writer, "I have brought you a drink of water."

"Ah," said Jesus. "I am quite thirsty. Thank you."

Jesus drank deeply.

"Jesus," whispered Writer, "I have done a terrible thing. It was I who fetched the thirty pieces of silver the priests paid Judas to betray you. It was a shameful thing. I have come to make amends. I can help you escape. I am the priests' assistant. I have lived here since just after my mother weaned me. I know all the secret passages."

"Thank you," said Jesus. "Tell me your name."

"My name is Writer."

"What a strange name! Your mother must have wanted you to learn to read and write."

"Yes, that's it. How did you know?"

"A lucky guess, I suppose. Tell me, did your mother's wish come true?"

"Why, yes it did," said Writer a little proudly. "The priests taught me to read and write."

"That's good," said Jesus. "It is no accident, then, that you are here."

"Enough about reading and writing," said Writer a bit impatiently. "We must act quickly. I'll leave now, but I'll come back in about an hour. I'll tell the guards the chief priest sent me to get you. The jailer knows me well. He'll not question me. I'm the one who brings food to the prisoners. Then when you're out of the cell . . ."

"No," Jesus interrupted, "I have a better plan."

"Oh?" said Writer.

"This is what you must do. No matter what happens, one week from today you must leave the house of the high priest, but when you leave never forget the good things they have given you. Despite all their misdeeds and despite their holding hands with the Romans, they have kept the faith alive and have passed it to you. Not only that, they have taught you to read and write. After you leave, you must go to Galilee where the gifts given to you are greatly needed. In Galilee you will find the one we call Simon Peter. Tell him I sent you. He will welcome you. You will also find my followers. They'll likely be huddled and hiding, but when you find them tell Peter and the others all of the things you have told me. Then ask them to tell you my story and to tell you the things I taught them. When you have heard my story, I want you to write it down so my story will be preserved for many generations. You must trust me. This is a better way than running to hide."

Writer started to protest, but Jesus held up his hand to stop him.

Just then the guard shouted through the door, "How much water can one man drink? It's me'll have to pitch his piss out the window."

"Coming," said Writer.

"Promise me you will write my story," said Jesus.

"I promise."

> Now the chief priests and the whole council were looking for testimony against Jesus to put him to death; but they found none. For many gave false testimony against him, and their testimony did not agree. Some stood up and bore false testimony against him saying, "We heard him say, 'I will destroy this temple that is made with hands, and in three days I will build another, not made with hands.'"

The Journalist

Immediately, while [Jesus] was still speaking [to disciples], Judas, one of the twelve, arrived; and with him a crowd with swords and clubs, from the chief priests and the scribes and the elders.

Now the betrayer had given them a sign, saying, "The one I shall kiss is the man; arrest him and lead him away under guard."

So when he came, he went up to at once, and said, "Rabbi!" and he kissed him.

Then they laid hands on him and arrested him.

But one of those who stood near drew his sword and struck the slave of the high priest, cutting off his ear.

Then Jesus said to them, "Have you come out with swords and clubs to arrest me? Day after day I was with you in the temple teaching and you did not arrest me. But let the scriptures be fulfilled."

All of them deserted him and fled.

A certain young man was following him, wearing nothing but a linen cloth. They caught hold of him, but he left the linen cloth and ran off naked.

The young man cursed and grabbed for his linen cloth. It was useless. Someone pushed him to the ground as the thief lost himself in the crowd. Except for his military training and his quick action in getting back on his feet, the young man would likely have been trampled by the mob. They were obviously out to see blood, and it might as well have been his blood . . . except that he was no messiah.

In the midst of the throng, if he was self-conscious about being naked, he showed no sign of it. It was as though he had been seen this way before. He did, however, stand still and let the mass of angry humanity pass around him. At the edge of the crowd, when several young girls pointed and giggled, he no more than glanced in their direction and started walking aimlessly.

Once away from the mindless swarm he found the streets of Jerusalem almost deserted. "It's useless," he said to himself. "The market is empty. There will be no one selling linen cloth . . . linen cloth or anything else."

Just then he heard someone say in a stage whisper, "Here, Mark. Over here."

It was a young woman's voice. How could anyone know his name? He knew no one in Jerusalem. The voice was coming from an alley.

"Over here, Mark. Your name is Mark, isn't it?"

"Yes, but how do you know my name? Do I know you?"

"No, but I know you, or, at least I know who you are," the voice said. "Here take this linen cloth. It's one of my father's. Put it on. We must talk."

Mark wrapped the cloth around his loins. "Who are you?" he asked.

"My name is Anna. I am the daughter of Jairus. A few years ago, as we now count time, Jesus restored my life."

"You mean he gave you new meaning in life? I hear he can do that."

"Well, that too, but, no. He brought me back from the dead?"[2]

"Get out! How could that be?"

"Yes, it's true, and, whatever else that means, it means I have seen time from beyond time. That's how I know your name and that's how I know you were not only in Viet Nam, you were there for the My Lai massacre . . . or shall be at My Lai, depending on how you see time."

"I was (or shall be) there."

"Tell me, did you (or will you) hear Lieutenant Calley give the order to fire?"

"I honestly don't know who gave the order or if anybody did. All I know is we all started shooting and when it was over everyone was dead. They were mostly unarmed women and children. The sight and sound of it haunted me for the rest of my life. Now, at the point of my own death, in a warp of time, I came here seeking forgiveness, but it looks like I got here too late. If the mob has its way, they'll be putting Jesus to death."

"I understand time warps," said Anna. "Only those who have known eternity can really understand time.

"After the war, what did you do in civilian life?" she asked.

"I was a journalist. Why?"

"I wanted to hear you say it. As it happens, we have great need of a journalist just now."

"How so?" asked Mark.

"When all of this is over, someone must write the story of Jesus. I'm positive that's why you are here.

"A few days from now, I'll introduce you to Simon Peter and the other disciples. Interview them. Get them to tell you the story of Jesus. The story of Jesus must be written, and it must be written by someone who knows what it is to stand naked with guilt in the face of injustice . . . to stand naked before injustice and then to taste the freedom of forgiveness."

---

2. See Mark 5:21–43 and Luke 8:40–55 neither of which records the girl's name.

Now the chief priests and the whole council were looking for testimony against Jesus to put him to death; but they found none. For many gave false testimony against him, and their testimony did not agree. Some stood up and bore false testimony against him saying, "We heard him say, 'I will destroy this temple that is made with hands, and in three days I will build another, not made with hands.'"

The Sins of the Great-Grandfathers:
A Tale of Exposure

"My father was a good man," said my great aunt Sallie. I was holding a skein of navy blue yarn over my outstretched twelve-year-old arms gently, swaying them back and forth in rhythm with her winding the yarn into a ball. Her long snow white hair, neatly twisted in a bun on the back of her head, glistened in the sunlight that streamed through the window as she sat in a wheelchair bent slightly forward at the shoulders under the weight of years and the inactivity left in the wake of a broken hip. Whether she fell and broke her hip or her hip grew brittle and caused her to fall was never determined. In all events, after her hip broke, she divided her time living graciously with relatives. Such institutions as nursing homes had not yet been conceived, at least not to the knowing of our family. For the handful of her latter years, for three months at a stretch, she lived in our guest room, graced our table, read widely with her magnifying glass held just inches above the page, spun and respun familiar family tales, shared her considerable wisdom, tatted lace for the pillow cases of generations yet unborn, and knitted our winter sweaters.

"If you'll hold this skein of yarn for me while I wind it into a ball, I'll give you the next nickel I find in the pig track," she had said.

From that cheerful promise often made, I, like my brothers and cousins, concluded early in childhood that pigs either have few nickels or carefully guard their loose change. Still, such tasks were a small price to pay for the delight of her presence and wisdom, to say nothing of her sweaters and tatting (though the latter only later came into our the range of our appreciation).

"I've never known a better man than my father," she repeated. "William Haygood Stanmore." She said it with a lilt of pride in her voice. "He was your great-grandfather, you know."

She paused to let me absorb the pride of it.

"But there's something you should know," she continued. "Though he was truly a good man, he owned slaves. Slavery was a great evil. It will be as Moses said," she said, picking up speed in the winding rhythm. "The sins of the fathers will be heaped on the heads of the children for the third and fourth generation."

She abruptly stopped her winding, paused again in her speech, then slowly continued both.

"Do you know what that means?"

Though it was a question, it was clear she would provide the answer with no prompting.

"That means you and your children will have to pay the for the sins of my father. I'm sorry, and I think, if in heaven he knows it, it grieves him, but it's true. I am the first generation after slavery, your mother is the second, you are the third, and your children will be the fourth. That means you and your children will have to pay for the sins of my father," she repeated.

Soon after that, the United States Supreme Court handed down its landmark decision in *Brown v. Board of Education.*

Just four years after that I packed my clothes in the footlocker Pappy brought home from World War II, loaded the footlocker in my mother's 1956 Chevrolet and drove with her sixty-five miles away from home to make my mark on Presbyterian College in Clinton, South Carolina. Having dropped me off, my mother drove the Chevrolet back home.

At Presbyterian College in the fall of 1958, the full impact of the Supreme Court decision in *Brown v. The Board of Education* had not even begun to be felt. At other colleges spotted here and there in the South, demonstrations demanding equal rights had begun. At Presbyterian, however, the innocents of the post-war years persisted apace for yet awhile. On the positive side, there was fraternity rush wherein we were made to feel like kings. On the other hand, there was "rat season" wherein freshmen were made to do such things as wear beanies, bow to the mailbox where upperclassmen mailed letters to their girlfriends, and run naked dodging through the backyards of the good people of Clinton all the way to the town square to sign the monument. In return for such raucous behavior we were given the privilege of polishing the upperclassmen's ROTC shoes and brass.

That such a way of life was about to come to an abrupt halt had not yet come clear to me when in mid-December of that year I returned home for the Christmas vacation.

To earn a few extra bucks during the break, I drove the old bill collector's route I had given up when I left home for college. The custom of bill collecting in our little town was time honored. It is true, a few but only a very few, of the people on my route were deadbeats. Those few had little or no intention of ever paying what they owed my father for the building materials and hardware he had sold them on credit. A small but important part of my job was to keep them reminded of their debt. For most of the people on whom I called, however, the practice was nothing more than my father, like many other merchants in town, providing an interest-free service to his customers who were either housebound or had no readily available transportation. From the time I was fourteen, the legal driving age in South Carolina at the time, until I left for Presbyterian College in the fall of 1958, every Friday after school and every Saturday morning I drove my father's pickup truck from house to house collecting payments of as little as fifty cents to as much as ten or, on rare occasions, twenty dollars. It was a good job. I was almost invariably received with hospitality and gratitude.

"How much is left on my bill?"

"It looks like you got it down to under ten dollars."

"I been thinking this old porch floor needs painting. Reckon your daddy would sell me a gallon of porch and deck enamel?"

"I'm sure he'd be pleased and grateful for the business."

"How about you bring it to me next week when you come this way? You can just add it to my bill, if your daddy don't mind."

"Yes, ma'am. You want it about the same color it is now."

"Little darker gray maybe, so it won't show dirt so bad."

"Yes, ma'am. Would you be needing a brush to put it on with and some mineral spirits to clean up after?"

"Got a brush from last time, but I'm glad you brought the mineral spirits to mind."

"Ok, that'll be a gallon of dark gray porch and deck enamel and a quart of mineral spirits. I'll make a note of it so I won't forget."

"If you don't mind, put the paint on the shaking machine and shake it up real good before you bring it so it won't be such a bother stirring it."

"Yes, ma'am. I'll be sure to shake it real good. Can I bring you anything else?"

"I don't think so right now. Better get the paint paid down a little first, but then I'd like to talk to you 'bout a new screen door. Can I git you a glass of ice tea? Made it fresh this mornin'."

"Why, thank you, ma'am. That'd be mighty nice."

"Ain't got no lemon but reach down there beside the steps and pinch you off a sprig of mint."

"I much prefer mint to lemon myself."

It truly was an age of innocence. One might say it was more like Mayberry than Mayberry.

When I made the collection rounds on the first Friday of Christmas break there was much handshaking and backslapping with Christmas cookies or fruitcake at almost every stop.

"No, sir, it's too early to tell, but it doesn't look like I'm going to be making anything like straight A's. That's my older brother. He's the smart one."

"No special girlfriend yet. Not many to choose from at P. C. Except for a few day students, it's an all boys school, but I manage to get over to Converse and up to Winthrop now and then."

"I like my roommates just fine. One is from Easley. The the other's from Charlotte."

"This is the best fruitcake I've tasted in I can't tell you how long."

With conversations like those at almost every house along the way, the collection route took much longer to make than usual. That coupled with the short days of December made it well after dark when I made my way to The Quarters and turned left on Washington Street for the last stop of the day. I wanted nothing so much as to get home for a quick change of clothes and a bite of supper before heading off to the party that had been planned for the class of '58. Everybody who had stayed home to work in the mills plus those of us who were home from college would be there. It would be the first time most of us had seen each other since the end of summer.

The Quarters was the polite name for the African American community in our town. It's a vestige of slavery days. What we yet called it just four years after the *Brown v. The Board of Education* decision should not be written on these pages. Washington Street, though it was lined with houses, was not so much a street as a pair of clay tracks between two ditches. It was nearly impassable after a rain. So far as I can recall, it never dawned on anyone that the streets of The Quarters should be improved by the town fathers, and they were all fathers at the time.

As it happens, the clay tracks that were Washington Street were not named to honor our first president, at least not directly. The two-track street was named for my client, who was named for the famous Booker T. Washington. My client, who had shortened his name to "Tee," ran The Half Moon Social Club, a juke joint at the end of the street that bore its proprietor's name.

I was tempted to skip the last stop. It was late, but more than that, I was all but certain I wouldn't get so much as a thin dime from Tee Washington. The balance on his account was eighty-six dollars and fifteen cents, exactly the same as it had been several months earlier when last I made the collection rounds. Tee Washington, however, was one of the very customers Pappy wanted to keep reminded of his debt so I dutifully turned the

Chevrolet pickup onto Washington Street, bumped my way to the end, and parked beside the half dozen or so cars of the early Friday night revelers.

In all the times I had called on Tee Washington at the Half Moon Social Club I had never encountered more than one or two customers at a time, and they were almost always the same old men who were there passing the afternoon drinking beer and playing checkers. This time it was different. When I got out of the truck, I could hear a Fats Domino tune playing on the jukebox. A string of multicolored Christmas lights lined the single door of the weathered clapboard building. A soft glow came from behind the lighted Pabst Blue Ribbon sign in the window.

Inside the Half Moon Social Club on the Friday before Christmas, three or four young couples were dancing with a passion I had never before seen. It took me off guard. I couldn't help but stand and stare. Before I caught myself and realized what I was doing, which couldn't have been more than a second or two, one of the dancers saw me and motioned with her head to the others in my direction. They all stopped dancing and made their way to stand beside the jukebox. They peered through the glass at the list of records to avoid looking at me. I moved toward the bar where Tee Washington was serving up drinks. By the time I got to the bar, as if on cue, the Fats Domino tune ended. There was stone silence.

"How you doin', Tee?" I said in a muffled tone. "Merry Christmas."

"Tee! Who you callin' Tee?" he retorted. "How old are you, boy?"

"Just turned nineteen."

"Then that'd be Mr. Washington to you, now wouldn't it? How much my bill?"

"Eighty-six dollars and fifteen cents."

He reached under the counter, retrieved a metal box, and counted out eighty-six dollars in well worn ones and fives. He then reached in his pocket and pulled out a dime and five pennies. He handed it to me and said, "I'll be needing a receipt."

I filled in the blanks on the receipt form: *Received of Tee Washington, eighty-six and 15/100 dollars*. I signed it, tore it out of the book, and handed it to him. He looked at it and handed it back.

"My name is *Mr.* Booker T. Washington."

I voided the receipt and wrote another: *Received of Mr. Booker T. Washington eighty-six and 15/100 dollars*. To my sure knowledge, it is the first time I ever called a black man *Mr.* He looked at the rewritten receipt, put it in his shirt pocket, and turned away with no further comment. The silence in the Half Moon Social Club echoed in my ears. "Thank you," I said weakly as I turned to leave.

He turned back sharply, and with fire in his eyes he said, "Boy, I don't know how you think you gonna get out of college. You don't learn very fast. That's *'Thank you, sir'* to you."

"Thank you, sir," I said as I made my way to the door. To my sure knowledge, it's the first time I ever called a black man *sir*.

As I walked out the door I heard a nickel drop in the jukebox then heard a Little Richard tune to which I had danced many times. Rather than sway to its beat, I all but ran to pickup. Though I didn't think of it at the time, the sins of my great-grandfather were chasing me like the hounds of Hades.

That was the last stop on the route. I got to my father's store just before closing time. I gave the money I had collected and my receipt book to the bookkeeper. As she reconciled the two, never one to mince words, she exclaimed in a loud voice, "How did you manage to get all this money from Tee Washington? Must have held him down and beat it out of him."

"Not a chance. All I can tell you is he was mad. It was like he was mad at me. I don't know why. I never did anything to him. He even wanted me to call him 'Mr.'"

"You didn't do it, did you?"

"What do you think? Mine was the only white face for a mile in any direction. What'd I ever do to him?"

Little did I know there was more to come on that fateful night.

On my way home to shower and get ready for the party, about halfway to our farm and maybe a mile or two out of town, I saw red lights flashing up the road. When I got to where they were, I recognized Bobby Taylor's patrol car. Bobby Taylor was the highway patrolman assigned to our area. There was also a wrecker from Jamerson's Garage. Zeke Jamerson had been in my class but dropped out of school to work in his father's garage. There was also the familiar dark green 1949 Pontiac hearse from the funeral home. The Pontiac hearse doubled as an ambulance. It was long before ambulance drivers were required to have special training. Ambulance service was provided by funeral directors. Bill Morris was so short and round he tucked a towel in his belt to keep the steering wheel from wearing out his pants while driving the ambulance in speeds nearing 100 miles per hour. He was leaned against the coach. The lights from the hearse were shining on a black man stretched out on the shoulder of the road. Zeke was down in the ditch hooking an old Ford to the tow cable of the wrecker.

I knew Bill Morris well. I had ridden with him from time to time on ambulance runs. About all we could do for anybody was to get them to the hospital as fast as we could. Sometimes he would let me drive the ambulance home from the hospital.

"What happened?" I asked Bill.

Indicating the man on the shoulder of the road, Bill said, "Looks like he run off the road and down in the ditch. Don't smell like he's drunk or nothin' like that. Must have fell asleep."

"Is he dead?"

"Nah."

"Aren't you going to take him to the hospital?"

"I'm waiting on the people from Hanson's to come over from Lancaster."

"It'll take'm a good half hour or forty-five minutes to get here, and it looks like he's hurt pretty bad."

"Oh, he ain't all that bad off. Head wounds just bleed a lot. If he was really bad off, I'd wrap him up good and take him, but as long it don't look like he's gonna die or nothin', we might as well wait and let his own kind take care of him. If word got out we was hauling n___s in our coach . . . . Well, let me put it this way. It wouldn't help business very much."

Just then, the man on the side of the road turned his head and opened his eyes to look at me and Bill.

In the distance I could hear a siren.

"That'd be the folks from Hanson's." Bill looked at his watch as he spoke. "They made pretty good time. Got here in thirty-five minutes from the time I called 'em. It's hard to beat them '48 Buick coaches, but I think I could beat him to the hospital any day of the week. The Pontiac's better in the curves. The Buick shocks is too soft, if you know what I mean."

I looked back at the man on the shoulder of the road. He didn't divert his gaze.

In a few minutes, two men from Hanson Funeral Home gently loaded the man on a stretcher, put the stretcher in the back of the black hearse, and locked it in place. As the driver walked around to his door, he paused and looked over at Bill and me. There was in his expression more insight than disdain.

"Well, boys, you know how it is," said Bill.

I made my way to my mother's car, sat there a few minutes, and for the second time that night felt the weight of my great-grandfather's sin chasing after me.

I peeled rubber trying to get away. It didn't work.

Francine The Dancing Queen

In the summer of 1956 a carnival came to our town for a two-night stand. Three weeks before the big event an advance man rode all over town in an old red convertible with a faded seductive likeness of Francine the Dancing Queen painted on each of its doors. He stapled posters on every light pole in town, or so it seemed. For three weeks, everywhere you looked, there was a picture of Francine.

I don't recall a carnival ever coming to our town before or since. Sure enough, as one might have guessed, that one came to our wee town at all meant they were more than a little desperate. Still, excitement was high, especially among the townsfolk who seldom got out of town. When opening day finally arrived, the latter group didn't seem to mind that everything about the carnival was faded, worn, chipped, and held together with bailing wire. Horses were missing from the merry-go-round, cars were missing from the ferris wheel, the cupie dolls and Teddy bears were shopworn, the record player blaring out carnival music repeatedly got stuck and skipped groves. Worst of all, the hotdog buns were cold and stale. None of that seemed to matter to those for whom magic was in the air.

Most impressive of all, at the end of a row of booths at which you could do such things as buy cotton candy or try your luck at shooting moving ducks or knocking over a stack of wooden milk bottles with a softball, as advertised, there was a faded purple tent with a giant likeness of Francine the Dancing Queen over the door. A barker stood just outside extolling Francine's beauty, charm, and mystique, assuring one and all that she was fresh off the boat having arrived only days before all the way from Paris, France just so she might appear in Great Falls, South Carolina. For a mere twenty-five cents you could get in the door to witness her moves at a distance. For fifty cents you could stand down front just beside the stage to see up close the eighth wonder of the world. "Please," he said, "only men can get in. No boys allowed. You must be eighteen years of age to enter the pleasure palace that is just through the curtain to my left."

My friends Larry Hager and John Quincy Greshem and I went to the carnival on opening night to see if it would be worthwhile taking dates the following night. We walked past the rundown rides, the row of chance-taking booths, and fast-food vendors to check out Francine the Dancing Queen. Looking around to see if any teachers or preachers were watching, we sidled up to the barker and held out our quarters. "How old are you boys?" the barker asked. John Quincy told him he was nineteen. Larry and I each said we were eighteen. All of us lied.

"Yeah, yeah," said the disbelieving barker as he took our money. "Stand near the back and if a policeman shows up slip out under the tent flap."

By the time the show started there were probably as many as twenty men in the tent. Maybe eight or ten were standing next to the stage. It was nothing more than a platform maybe six or eight inches off the ground. Others crowded just behind those in front being held at bay by a ratty velvet rope stretched across the tent. John Quincy, Larry, and I stood near the back like we had been told.

The show started with great fanfare from the barker. "Gentlemen, it is my distinct pleasure and privilege to present for your manly entertainment, choreographed to excite your manly instincts, straight from Paris, France, the one, the only, the beautiful, the exotic, Francine the Dancing Queen."

With that, recorded music of the bump and grind variety blared over loudspeakers on each end of the stage.

When Francine appeared from behind a curtain, it was clear she was, shall we say, a bit past her prime as an exotic dancer. In fact, if she ever looked like her pictures on the doors of the convertible, the posters, or on the canvas above the tent flap, those days were past.

Still, she did have the right moves. When she had off all her clothes except for a G-string and two tassels, she could twirl the tassels round and round first in the same direction, then in two different directions, and then reverse them to twirl in the opposite directions. Men in the front got so excited they began throwing coins on the stage.

Then a man, he must have been a plant, held out a dollar bill. She came over, took the dollar bill and tucked it in her G-string. She then reached down, unzipped his pants, and slipped her hand inside. Her facial expression let you know she was impressed with what she found. In a seductive stage whisper she asked the man if he didn't want to come to her trailer after the show.

Other men on the front began holding up dollar bills.

When the show was over, Larry, John Quincy, and I beat a hasty retreat. We ducked to the side of the tent to be sure no one we knew saw us leaving. There, beside the tent, was the old red convertible we had seen before. Beside the convertible was a rundown house trailer. A little girl of maybe four or five was sitting on the steps of the trailer. She was holding a doll.

As we walked pass the trailer, Francine appeared from behind the tent wearing a robe over her G-string and tassels. One of the men from the front row was with her. The little girl ran up to Francine holding up her arms. "Mommy, Mommy," the little girl said with excitement.

"Not now, Gracie, Mommy's working."

Strange how I still remember the little girl's name was Gracie.

Next night I didn't take a date to the carnival. Neither did John Quincy or Larry.

six

But What Does It Mean?
(Mark 16:1–8)

Notes on the Text

AS IS POINTED OUT briefly in the introduction, among the silences in the Gospel of Mark, the present text presents the *opus magnum*. That is to say, it is all but universally agreed among New Testament scholars (as well as among serious and even casual observers) that Mark, whoever he (or she?) might have been, ended the gospel narrative at 16:8. In Mark's account, the women, having heard the announcement, flee the tomb in fear and amazement and tell no one what they have seen and heard. The balance of the book as it appears in the Christian cannon of scripture is a late addition or, much more likey, a series of late additions.

In Matthew, after the announcement of Jesus' resurrection, as the women are running to tell the others, Jesus himself greets the women. There is also in Matthew the story of a conspiracy to silence the guards who might otherwise have confirmed the witness of the women. Moreover, Matthew famously includes what has come to be called The Great Commission wherein Jesus gives the church its marching orders. Luke has Peter, when he is told by the women what they have seen and heard, running to see for himself. That scene is followed in Luke by Jesus walking with strangers on the road to Emmaus. The strangers recognize him in the breaking of bread. Luke then tells of Jesus appearing to the disciples and giving last minute instructions before they witness him ascending into heaven. John, so unlike the others, has two endings that have tantalized interpreters for generations. In the first, the risen Jesus appears first to Mary Magdalene and then on two occasions makes dramatic appearances to disciples who are holed up behind locked doors. In the second ending, John has Jesus appear first to seven disciples, then to Peter, and at last to John, the author of the book.

Not so, this Mark person. He would have none of it and it must be remembered, among the gospel narratives in the Christian cannon of scriptures, Mark was the first to commit it all to writing. In its original form Mark ends the narrative with striking drama by leaving readers to ponder with the terrified women what it means that Jesus has been raised from the dead.

As in previous chapters, the effort in the tales that follow is not to end that discussion but to enliven it. Through these stories readers are encouraged, on the one hand, to broaden an appreciation for the significance of the central message of the Christian gospel and, on the other hand, to focus more narrowly on the significance of resurrection hope in the ongoing practice of the Christian faith and its mission. Once again, in the first two tales I enter the text and provide fanciful fictitious material. The other two pieces are testimony to my father's radical, yet ever so earthy, practice of faith and ministry as that practice bore unshakable testimony to his belief in resurrection hope.

Joshua and the Women of Easter

> *When the sabbath was over, Mary Magdalene, Mary the mother*
> *of James, and Salome brought spices, so that they might go up*
> *and anoint him. And very early on the first day of the week,*
> *when the sun had risen, they went to the tomb. They had been*
> *saying to one another, "Who will roll away the stone for us from*
> *the entrance to the tomb?" When they looked up, they saw that*
> *the stone, which was very large, had already been rolled back.*
> *As they entered the tomb, they saw a young man, dressed in a*
> *white robe, sitting on the right side, and they were alarmed. But*
> *he said to them, "Do not be alarmed; you are looking for Jesus of*
> *Nazareth, who was crucified. He has been raised, he is not here.*
> *Look, there is the place they laid him. But go, tell his disciples*
> *and Peter that he is going ahead of you to Galilee; there you will*
> *see him, just as he told you." So they went out and fled from the*
> *tomb, for terror and amazement had seized them; and they said*
> *nothing to anyone for they were afraid.*

Instinctively, as the three women left the tomb, they covered their
faces with shawls. With heads bowed, they looked at the ground as they
walked in silence. The crunch of stones under their feet was the only sound
they heard. None dared speak. Soon, however, as they approached the
city, they were able to blend in with the crowd as shoppers and vendors
set about tending the day's wheeling and dealing. Strange, thought Salome,
how quickly everything returns to business as usual. It's as though nothing
at all happened here in the last few days . . . no bloodletting, no gore, no
crimes of temple and state.

Finally, Mary the mother of James turned to the other Mary and said
in a hushed but angry tone, "What does this mean?"

"I have no idea," whispered the Magdalene, the woman from whom
Jesus had cast seven demons.

"Mean? It means the Romans will blame us for stealing the body," said
Salome not at all quietly.

"Shhhh. Maybe we did," said the mother of James. "No one knows
where the men are or what they've been up to. Maybe they did steal the
body. I wouldn't put it past them."

"Oh, I doubt it," said Mary Magdlene. "They're probably just hiding
someplace for fear what happened to Jesus will happen to them."

Then, as they were approaching the gate to the temple grounds, they heard a familiar voice. "Alms for the poor . . . alms for the poor. Can't anyone spare a few coins for a poor blind beggar?"

Joshua was a fixture on the temple grounds.

"Well, Joshua," said the Magdalene, "you know we don't have any money, but come with me. When we left, Lydia said she would have breakfast for us when we came home . . . not that we feel like eating. I'm sure there's enough to share."

"Ah, it's you, Mary," said Joshua who recognized her voice. "It's awful what they did to your friend. What a sham. He never did anyone any harm."

As Salome put Joshua's dirty hand on her shoulder she said not sarcastically, "Count it a blessing you didn't have to see it."

He followed the three women to the Magdalene's home. When they got there, Lydia met them at the door. She held a baby on her hip. Several months earlier Jesus had found Lydia on the streets pitifully trying in vain to sell her body to Roman soldiers. Pregnant, alone and with no husband, her father disowned her. Prostitution was her only option. Roman soldiers had been her best customers, but she had begun to show, and no one wanted her for fear she would blame the child on them. Jesus brought her to the Magdalene's home and asked Mary to take her in. To Lydia, Mary had become as both mother and sister.

"Come in," said Lydia. "What was it like at the tomb? Was there an odor?"

In some ways Lydia was more like a child than a mother.

"Odor? There was no odor. He wasn't even there."

"What do you mean?"

The house smelled of freshly baked bread.

"I mean the body was gone."

"Gone? How could that be?"

"I have no idea. All we know is a man dressed in white said he would meet us in Galilee."

"Who would meet you in Galilee?"

"I guess he meant Jesus."

"Jesus is dead. I saw him myself."

The Magdalene, handing Joshua a basin and a towel, led him behind a screen. "Here," she said, "wash yourself before we eat."

"I must stink," he said.

"A little," she said.

"A lot," said the mother of James, who was never one to mince words.

When they had sat down, for a while no one said anything. Finally Salome said rather gruffly, "Well?"

"Well, what?" said the Magdalene.

"Well, are we going to Galilee or not, and what do we tell the disciples?"

"Tell the disciples? If we can find them we tell them what we have seen and heard, but don't be foolish," said the mother of James. "There's no use to go to Galilee. Jesus is dead. We washed the blood and filth from his body. We saw the pallor of his skin and his eyes rolled back in their sockets. He's not going to meet anyone in Galilee or anywhere else."

For a moment no one said anything. Then Salome, almost sheepishly, reminded them that Jesus himself had said it would be as the man in white said.

"I don't care what he said," said the mother of James. "Dead is dead."

There was another pause. At last the Magdalene said, "I can't speak for you, but I, for one, am going to find the disciples. I'm going to tell them what we have seen and heard, and then I'm going to Galilee to see for myself."

Joshua, who until then had said nothing since they sat at table, spoke up and said, "Well, if you're going to Galilee to find Jesus, you better take Lydia and me with you."

"Why?" asked the Magdalene. "What help can you be?"

"Not much, I suppose, but from what I hear, when you get to Galilee if you're in the company of an unwed mother with her baby and a blind beggar who stinks, he'll be more likely to find you."

Very Early on the Second Day of the Week

When the sabbath was over, Mary Magdalene, Mary the mother of James, and Salome brought spices, so that they might go up and anoint him. And very early on the first day of the week, when the sun had risen, they went to the tomb. They had been saying to one another, "Who will roll away the stone for us from the entrance to the tomb?" When they looked up, they saw that the stone, which was very large, had already been rolled back. As they entered the tomb, they saw a young man, dressed in a white robe, sitting on the right side, and they were alarmed. But he said to them, "Do not be alarmed; you are looking for Jesus of Nazareth, who was crucified. He has been raised, he is not here. Look, there is the place they laid him. But go, tell his disciples and Peter that he is going ahead of you to Galilee; there you will see him, just as he told you." So they went out and fled from the tomb, for terror and amazement had seized them; and they said nothing to anyone for they were afraid.

The women, though close friends, agreed they wanted nothing so much as to be alone, each to deal with their shared unspeakable grief in her own way. For Mary the mother of James, it was sitting in a darkened room in stunned silence. For Salome, it was fiercely cleaning every nook and cranny of her already spotless hovel. For the Magdalene, it was collapsing in tears on her mat where she soon escaped into a deep, deep sleep of the sort where dreams flow freely.

In her dream, Mary saw herself on a path that wound its way up a hill, the top of which was beyond her sight. Coming down the hill to meet her was a man she thought she recognized. When he drew closer she said, "Simon, is that you?"

"It is I," said Simon Peter as he reached out his hand. "Come with me."

Together they walked to the top of the hill from which the view of the valley below was clear and beautiful. It was green and lush with all manner of vegetation set against a backdrop of sky streaked with bright yellow rays dancing across snow-white clouds. On the floor of the valley was set a banquet table that stretched farther than the eye could see.

"Come with me," Simon repeated. "There's a place for you at the table."

As they approached the table Mary could see there were men, women, girls, and boys of every size, color, and shape all dressed in white, seated on both sides of the table laughing and talking. The women and girls were all, every one, ever so beautiful. The men and boys were as handsome as the women and girls were beautiful. Waiters, also dressed in white, were darting to and fro serving a feast of red wine and all manner of delicacies.

As they passed along the path behind the table dodging the waitstaff, Mary said to Simon Peter, "Simon, who are these?"

"These are those who reached the age of three score years and ten or more."

Across the path from the table were animals of every kind. The cats and dogs were playing with each other, and the wolves and lambs were napping side by side.

"And who are these?" asked Mary, gesturing to the other diners as they continued to walk beside the table.

"These are the ones who died in tsunamis, hurricanes, tornados, and floods," said Simon.

"And these, who are these?"

"These are the ones who met their fate by terrible accident."

On and on they walked. From time to time two people would get up from the table and playfully make their way into the lush garden. Most times it was a man and woman. Occasionally it was two men or two women.

"Where are they going?" asked Mary.

"Where do you think?" said Simon. "But don't worry. They'll be back for dessert."

"Oh," said Mary.

She began looking at the men in a whole new light.

"And these?" she asked gesturing toward the table but glancing briefly to the other side of the path to watch as calves, lions, and fatlings were together being led by a little child.

"These are the ones who died from acts of genocide, and up there are the ones who died in acts of terror, and up there are the victims of war, and over there are the prey of drug lords."

"And these, who are these?"

"These are the ones who contracted preventable diseases, and these the ones who died for want of health care, and these from starvation in the face of plenty, and these are the ones who died in utero."

All along they had to dodge the waitstaff, first bumping into a waiter carrying a tray laden with rich food and then a busboy carrying dirty dishes.

"Notice the names on the waitstaff's badges," Simon Peter whispered in the ear of his old friend.

Some of the names didn't mean anything to Mary, but there were many names that did mean something to her . . . enough that she began to get the picture. They had names like Ivan and Caesar and Edie and Mussolini; Osama, Moammar, Atilla, Rush, Sarah, Newt, and George; and, as if for comic relief, there was a busboy named Hagar.

At last they came to the head of the table. From the one seated at the head she heard the old familiar voice say to her, "Mary, meet me in Galilee, but first, take your place at the table even if ever so briefly."

As Simon and Mary turned to leave, Mary said to Simon Peter, "What is this?"

"This is the Feast of the First Day," said Simon. "For six days, as days on earth are counted, the myriads of the redeemed, all dressed in white, live in joy and peace. On the first day, again, as days on earth are counted, everyone gathers for the Feast of the First Day. Here they are hosted by the Lamb of God and served by tyrants and despots who, like all others, have been redeemed and made whole.

"I'll show you to your seat."

On the table in front of an empty chair was a name plate carved in stone. The name carved in the stone was Mary of Magdala.

As she was about to be seated, a waiter appeared as if from nowhere and said, "My name is Pilate. Adolph and I will be serving of you today."

As Mary sat down, suddenly the waitstaff, as they continued to serve the redeemed, began to sing in perfect harmony, "For the Lord God omnipotent reigneth."

The diners joined in unison, "Hallelujah! Hallelujah! Hallelujah!"

Mary woke herself singing in her sleep, "Hallelujah, Hallelujah . . ."

She sprang from her mat. When she had splashed water on her face, she packed several loaves of bread in a cloth and went to fetch the other Mary and Salome.

And so it is that at dawn on the second day of the week, three women set off on a journey.

A Thief in the Night

In the early spring of 1958 Billy Neely broke into Pappy's store. It happened in the dark of night. I remember it was the spring of 1958 because that's the year Sparky graduated from MIT and I graduated from Great Falls High School. Sparky is my older brother.

Soon after midnight on the night in question, Pappy got a call from Hugh Gatlin, the chief of police in our little town.

"Lowry," said Chief Gatlin. The men in town largely called Pappy by his last name only and when the pronounced his name it sounded more like *Larry* than *Lowry*. "Lowry," said Chief Gatlin, "Fox Trot Alan caught Billy Neely in your store. Fox Trot was on routine patrol . . . ." The chief liked to use words like *routine patrol*. It made him sound like Sergeant Joe Friday on *Dragnet*. "Fox Trot Alan was on routine patrol, and when he rode by your store he saw what looked like a flashlight shining inside the window. When he checked it out he saw Billy Neely in there and caught him red-handed looking through the merchandise just like he was on a shopping spree or something.

"You know Billy Neely," the chief went on. "He's one of Brenda Neely's boys."

Brenda Neely was a single mother with a yard full of children and was down on her luck. Her husband, like many men in those days, just left home one day and never came back. Speculation around town was that he was probably in Texas someplace.

"I see," said Pappy. "How old did you say the boy is?"

"I didn't say," said Chief Gatlin again trying to sound like Sergeant Joe Friday. "He looks to be about eleven or twelve years old."

"I see," Pappy said.

Pappy often said *I see*. I think he said it because he mostly really did understand what was happening but also because it gave him a chance to think for a second or two before he spoke further.

"What'd you do with him?" Pappy asked.

"Fox Trot took him to Chester to the county jail."

"I see."

The morning after Billy Neely broke into Pappy's store and Fox Trot Alan hauled him off twenty miles away to the Chester County Jail, we all got up as usual. Banks and I fed the livestock while Pappy shaved and Mom cooked breakfast. Banks is my younger brother. After breakfast, as was his unshakable custom, Pappy read from the Revised Standard Version Bible.

Reading from the Revised Standard Version of the Bible rather than the King James Version was yet in 1958 considered to be a little on the wild side, but Pappy was well versed in matters biblical so could see the advantage in a more up-to-date translations.

I don't remember exactly where he was reading at the time, but I do remember on the morning after Billy Neely broke in his store, Pappy broke with his custom of reading straight through the Bible and skipped to Matthew 25. When he got to the place where it says Jesus said, "I was in prison and you came to me," he paused for a second and raised his left eyebrow as he was wont to do when there was a point to be made. Then, when he got to the place where it says Jesus said, "In as much as you have done it to one of the least of these, you have done it to me," he stopped reading, raised his left eyebrow again, closed the Bible, and led the family prayer. In addition to praying for Sparky at MIT, me and Banks in our respective schools, Mom in her teaching, and a half dozen or so others for whom he had particular concern, Pappy prayed that morning for Billy Neely.

After breakfast, Pappy got in his Chevrolet pickup truck and drove the twenty miles or so to the county seat. His old friend and business partner Judge Timmons was the county judge in those days. Pappy drove straight to Judge Timmons's house.

"Judge," Pappy said, "you've got an eleven or maybe twelve-year-old boy in your jail by the name of Billy Neely. I want you to sentence him to live with me and Beck and the boys for a while."

"He must have done something pretty bad," the judge is reported to have said as he laughed outloud. The judge knew well what life was like in our home. He had been there many times and as often as not he, along with Mrs. Timmons, had his feet under my mother's table.

Pappy didn't laugh.

"Fox Trot Alan caught him in my store last night."

Pappy raised his left eyebrow when he said it. Of course, I was not there actually to hear that Pappy didn't laugh and see him raise his left eyebrow, but I know full well it did happen. Pappy's raised left eyebrow was a gesture worth far more than a thousand words in any known language. That gesture could, depending on the occasion, mean anything from utter disdain for what had just been said to endless pride in the person who just spoke.

"You just go down to the jail and get him," said the judge. "I'll sign the order as soon as I get to my office. In the meantime, I'll call 'em at the jail and tell 'em you're comin'."

That's the story of how Billy Neely came to live with us from then until he graduated from Great Falls High School. The day Pappy brought Billy Neely to live with us he didn't own anything but one pair of high-water pants: No shoes, no shirt, no toothbrush, no nothing except for one pair of high-water pants. By Judge Townson's order, he had to live with us a given number of months. After that, by invitation, he was free to live with us as often as he chose, which was pretty much all the time. He helped feed the livestock, gather eggs, and cut the grass. He also worked in Pappy's store after school and on Saturdays for which he was paid a fair wage. At first, Mom dressed him in my hand-me-downs, but soon he was able to delight in buying his own clothes. I don't remember even once that his manners or language usage were corrected, but Bank's manners and my manners as well as our language were corrected in Billy's hearing with more regularity than usual. He was all ears and a quick study.

Stories about Billy Neely living with us are legion, such as, for example, the story of when Billy, who had never before been farther away from home than the county jail, drove with Pappy and Mom and Banks in Mom's 1956 Chevrolet all the way from Great Falls, South Carolina to Boston, Massachusetts. They went to witness Sparky graduate from MIT. In the way of middle children, I stayed behind to tend the store and feed the livestock. I can only guess about what impression Billy Neely left on Boston, but I do know when they got back I asked Billy what he liked most about Boston. He told me with great animation about how in Boston in the public bathrooms they have machines on the wall where all you have to do is push a button and hot air comes out to dry your hands. According to Billy, in Boston you can even turn the nozzle on those same machines and dry your face.

It was about the time Billy graduated from high school that Pappy sold his business. Coincidently, soon after that the textile mills in our town closed. Soon after that, most of the businesses in town were forced to close as well. Like for so many once vibrant little towns like ours, there was little opportunity left for anyone, young or old. So like almost all young people, Billy had to leave town to seek his fortune. After that we pretty much lost touch with him.

Many years later, however, Billy showed up at our mother's door. It was during Holy Week of 1990 when we had all gathered for Pappy's funeral. None of us had seen Billy in all that time, but somehow he heard about Pappy's death and came to grieve deeply with the rest of us. He had with him his wife, a lovely and gracious woman, and two boys who were about half grown. They were all dressed fashionably. We learned he had risen through the ranks from a laborer in a warehouse in a nearby city to become foreman and dispatcher with many people working under his supervision. Billy and his wife owned a house in the suburbs, and the boys were doing well in school.

At Mom's insistence, after the other guests had left, Billy and his family stayed to have dinner with our family. As it happened, while food was being put on the buffet, there came a moment of wonder and grace that I'm profoundly grateful to have observed. The younger of Billy's sons was eyeing one of Mom's figurines as though his hands were itching to touch it. The little guy glanced to see if Billy were watching. As it happened, Billy was watching. Billy didn't say a word. He just raised his left eyebrow. The boy put his hands in his pockets.

Calves for Nayatoda

My brothers and I know very little about our father's experiences in World War II. He almost never spoke of such things. Most of what we know we learned either from our mother or by accident. For example we know he and the troops under his command were at the Battle of the Bulge. We know that because it's where he lost a fair amount of his hearing to what his doctor called "gunner's ear." We also know he was present for the liberation of a German interment camp. We know that because, by accident, I came across some photos he had taken of nude skin-and-bone bodies stacked like firewood just beside a fence topped with barbed wire. We also learned from our mother that just after the war ended he came upon some of the men in his command executing German prisoners of war. As a result of the latter experiences he came firmly to believe in the utter futility of war since, in his mind, the difference in his friends and his enemies was more quantitative than qualitative.

My father's favorite hymn goes like this:

> There were ninety and nine that safely lay
> in the shelter of the fold;
> but one was left in the hills far away,
> far off from the gates of gold,
> away on the mountains wild and bare,
> away from the tender shepherd's care,
> away from the tender shepherd's care.

He learned that hymn from his grandfather, the Rev. Milton Randolph Kirkpatrick. Milton Randolph Kirkpatrick used the hymn to keep rhythm while splitting firewood. According to family lore, to split firewood, my great-grandfather drove a steel wedge into a log using a ten-pound sledge-hammer with a four-foot handle. When my father was a young teen, his grandfather convinced my father that the surest sign of manhood was being able to drive a steel wedge into a log using a ten-pound sledgehammer with a four-foot handle. Like his grandfather before him, while swinging a sledgehammer, my father kept rhythm singing "The Ninety and Nine." Our father, again like his grandfather, passed the art on to his sons.

> Lord, thou hast here thy ninety and nine;
> are they not enough for thee?
> But the shepherd made answer: this of mine

has wandered away from me;
and though the road be rough and steep,
I go to the desert to find my sheep,
I go to the desert to find my sheep.

My brothers and I split a fair amount of firewood proving our manhood. In the process the parable of the Lost Sheep was so seared into the front of memory that, without a doubt, it became part of the fabric of our identity just as it was at the heart of Pappy's sure belief in Jesus as well as part of his very being.

Ballad-like, the hymn goes on for several verses and then concludes:

And the angels echoed around the throne,
"Rejoice, for the Lord brings back his own!"
"Rejoice, for the Lord brings back his own!"

One night, maybe five or six years after the war, at supper Pappy said he had heard from Mary Wright. He said in her letter she mentioned a young man by the name of Nayatoda who wanted to go to seminary but didn't have the necessary funds. Mary Wright and her husband were the last Presbyterian missionaries to leave Japan after the United States declared war on that rogue island nation. Mr. Wright died in their Charleston home during the war. Mrs. Wright was the first Presbyterian missionary to return to Japan after the war. Our parents cherished their friendship and admired them greatly.

That night at supper Pappy went on to say he had done some figuring. According to his calculations, if the market for beef held, the price of two healthy, well-fed year-old, half-breed bulls, at the current rate of exchange, would pay for that young man's seminary education for one year. He then wondered outloud if my brother Sparky and I would be willing to take on the task of raising two bull calves for that purpose. I was about eleven. Sparky is three years older. Our brother, Banks, was too young for the project.

Sparky and I agreed. How much our willingness to take on such a task was related to the parable of the Lost Sheep being part of the fabric of our psyche cannot be determined. Without a doubt, however, there is a straight line connecting that parable, Pappy's war experience, his passion for educating first one and then many Japanese seminary students, and his strong desire to involve his sons in the project.

Raising half-breed dogies is no small task but at the time they were cheap and they were plentiful. It was the practice then, as perhaps it is now, for dairy farmers in our area, when their herds were deemed large enough, to breed their Guernsey heifers to beef stock, thus producing calves suitable for the beef cattle market. At the same time, the farmers' young dairy cows were made ready to produce milk. When those calves were a week or two old, they would be separated from the herd and either raised separately for market or sold on the cheap to neighbors who were willing to go to considerable trouble necessary to raise them. For many months, twice a day nippled buckets had to be serialized and powdered formula had to be mixed in exact proportion in water that had been warmed to the exact temperature of a mother cow's body heat. The mixture then had to be delivered to the calves before it cooled. Moreover, while the evening feeding was during daylight hours, since the process usually took place during the school year, the morning feeding was invariable before sunup. This went on for three years during which my brother and I raised three calves each for a total of six calves. It was an early lesson in the cost of discipleship. Still Nayatoda's tuition was paid, in return for which we received thoughtful notes of thanks.

Many years later, when I was an up-and-coming young Presbyterian pastor, I got an enthusiastic call one night from my mother saying Nayotado would be visiting in their home for a few days. As moderator of the Presbyterian Church of Japan he would be in this country serving as a fraternal delegate to the then Presbyterian Church in the United States.

Just like in my father's favorite hymn, I could hear the angels echoing 'round the throne.